F   76399

RITCHIE

The payback

DATE DUE

NOV 4 '93	MAY 2 '00		
APR 26 '95	SEP 12 '00		
NOV 20 '95	OCT 3 '00		
JAN 21 '96	OCT 18 '00		
FEB 5 '98	FEB 21 02		
FEB 12 '99	SEP 28 '05		
MAR 2 '99			
MAR 15 '99			
SEP 9 '99			
SEP 29 '99			
DEC 15 99			
APR 28 '07			

DEMCO

THE PAYBACK

Also by the author

Over on the Lonesome Side

THE PAYBACK

James A. Ritchie

Walker and Company
New York

To Marla, Mary Kay, Sarah, Jeremiah, Nolan,
and Brennan. And to all those others
who believe in One True Love.

First published in the United States of America in 1992
by Walker Publishing Company, Inc.

Published simultaneously in Canada by Thomas Allen & Son
Canada, Limited, Markham, Ontario

Library of Congress Cataloging-in-Publication Data
Ritchie, James A.
The payback / James A. Ritchie.
171 p.   cm.
ISBN 0-8027-1233-9
I. Title.
PS3568.I814P38   1992
F   813'.54—dc20   92-21652
CIP

Printed in the United States of America

2   4   6   8   10   9   7   5   3   1

AUTHOR'S NOTE

The characters of Lieutenant Masterson, Ike Brown, Craven Lee, P. A. Gushurst, William Conners, James W. Wood, Lucretia (Aunt Lou) Marchbanks, Jack Langrishe, and Sheriff Seth Bullock, among others, are actual historical figures who lived in and around the town of Deadwood.

The names of the mining claims and the methods used in operating them, as well as the amounts of gold they yielded, also can claim historical accuracy.

The theaters, boardinghouses, hotels, and brothels existed as depicted, and Deadwood was one of the wildest towns in the Old West.

Wild Bill Hickok was killed there, Calamity Jane and Poker Alice were frequent visitors, and to this day Deadwood is a town unique in the events recorded there, and in the people who have called it home.

THE PAYBACK

CHAPTER 1

I RODE into Cheyenne with two dollars and change in my pocket. That mightn't sound like much, but I've seen the time when I'd have gladly herded sheep to get it. In Cheyenne, however, I was soon to learn that two dollars and change would barely pay for a good meal and a drink.

The city was all a-bustle, filled to overflowing with miners and would-be miners, every last one of them in a tizzy to leave Cheyenne and head for the Black Hills. Many had already been there, only to have soldiers from Fort Laramie escort them out with a stern warning not to return.

But where there's gold to be had, people are bound to go—army or no army. The Black Hills are sacred to the Sioux, and more than a few miners had been killed and scalped; but even that wasn't enough to keep them out.

Me, I'd been around gold a few times in my life, knew a good bit about finding it and getting it out of the ground, but I'd never thought of myself as a miner. Come to think of it, I never had any desire to get rich, either. That alone separated me from most of Cheyenne.

I was a cattle rancher, and that was the life I loved. Or had, until my luck ran out. It takes years of work and a wagonload of money to build a good ranch. Me and Mary Kay put in both, and we built the prettiest ranch in Colorado.

Then the anthrax came along and wiped out four years' work in two months. Hundreds of cattle died. Hundreds of others had to be killed and their carcasses burned. Then the bank foreclosed on the land.

Nobody—except Mary Kay—ever said I was anything but rawboned and tough, but losing that ranch near put me

1

under. Mary Kay is no bigger than a minute, but when all I wanted to do was quit, she put her tiny hands on her hips, flashed fire out of those beautiful green eyes, and chewed me up one side and down the other.

It made me ashamed of myself. There I was, married to the most beautiful woman who ever lived, and her six months pregnant with my child, and I was crying in my beer. So I stood up on my hind legs and started looking around for a way to start over. That's when word of a gold strike in the Black Hills spread across the country like a prairie fire.

I was reluctant to go at first, and it took Mary Kay's temper to light a fire under me and get me moving.

"James Darnell," she said, "sometimes you're a bigger knothead than any spur-scared mustang in the country. You don't want to leave because I'm pregnant, but let me tell you something. Women have been having babies for thousands of years, and the only help we ever needed from a man you've already done. Besides, I've talked to your father, and he said I was more than welcome to stay there for as long as it takes you up north."

"What about Rachel?"

"She's a wonderful woman—your father couldn't have found a better wife. The only thing left to do is to get you out of here."

She softened then and put her arms around me. "I know how losing the ranch hurt you," she said. "But I also know that isn't the real problem. You feel like you've let me and the baby down. That stubborn pride of yours isn't going to let you rest until you've found a way to earn a living. I'd love you just as much if we had to beg on the street for the rest of our lives, but that isn't your way, and I love that about you, too.

"So stop worrying about me and the baby. We'll be fine. You pack a bag, or roll your blankets, or whatever it is you have to do, and get going."

So that's the way it was. I stayed around just long enough

to move Mary Kay in with Pa and his new wife, then straddled Cap and rode north. Pa had a bit of money put back for hard times, and he tried to stake me, but I turned him down flat. Pa had his own banker to pay each month, and while the anthrax hadn't hit his herd as hard as mine, he was still going to need his savings to stay afloat.

I left Colorado with a twenty-dollar gold piece in my pocket, a spanking new sheepskin coat to keep me warm, and a fine horse under me. After some of the times I'd been through, riding along like that seemed almost luxurious.

Of course, once I spent the two dollars left in my pocket I'd be broke, but so what? That's the nice thing about being broke . . . there's nowhere to go but up. As I said, in Cheyenne two dollars and change wouldn't buy a *good* meal, but it would pay for beef and beans, so the first thing I did was find a saloon that sold them cheap. Then I started looking around for the right ladder to climb.

For two days I had no luck. Now, I'm not so smart as some, but I've a strong back, and after a time someone noticed and gave me a job. It didn't pay much, but it was enough to put Cap in a livery, and me in the loft above him. By limiting myself to two skimpy meals a day, I could even put back two bits toward a prospecting outfit.

Ordinarily, that would have been fine. Spend a couple of months putting together an outfit, then work my way into the Black Hills and find a claim that hadn't been staked. But having a pregnant wife back in Colorado made a difference. The thought of taking a moment longer than necessary made me cringe all over.

The odds were I'd be gone months, no matter how much luck I had. Every extra day tacked onto that looked like a year. One way or another, I had to speed things along.

But like a damn fool, I took what little money I had and found a small poker game, thinking to fill my poke in a hurry. There's a couple of sayings the cardsharps have, and I ignored them both. The first is, Never play poker if you can't afford to lose, and the second is, Scared money can't win.

I lost all I had. When I left the game there wasn't enough money in my pocket to buy more than two beers. With that in mind, I walked down to Chelcy's, sat down in a chair with my back to the wall, and sipped my first beer.

Mary Kay didn't hold with drinking, and I wasn't much on it myself. But now and then a cold beer goes down mighty smooth. That one didn't. All I could think of was Mary Kay waiting for me, and her belly growing every day.

Then Old Man Trouble started a game all his own, and like usual, he dealt me in.

It was the first week of November 1875, and it was colder than blue blazes. Most everybody not ready for bed had crowded into the saloons, and Chelcy's was no exception. Four would-be miners sat at a table near me, and they were talking up a storm about the Black Hills.

Now, almost everybody talked about the Black Hills and about the gold waiting to be picked up there, but these folks were talking about the outfits they intended to buy and just how much it would cost them.

That was fine, too. Where they made their mistake was taking out their money and counting it before God and everybody. Only a wet-behind-the-ears tenderfoot didn't know there are two things you never do in a saloon. You never mention a good woman, and you never, *never* flash your money roll.

Like I said, Chelcy's was crowded. Maybe sixty people lined the bar or sat around the tables, and I knew there was bound to be a few who'd take one look at all that money and start planning how to steal it.

At various times I'd been a marshal, a Wells Fargo guard, and a deputy sheriff. I'd learned the hard way to smell trouble, and now the odor was strong.

Out of habit, I took to looking around the saloon. In two shakes of a lamb's tail, I had spotted a likely pair of thugs.

They were seated at a table halfway across the room from the miners, but they were watching him count that money the way a hawk watches a mouse.

They were both big men, heavy-bodied, wide-shouldered, strong looking. Both were dressed in typical miner fashion, and they looked enough alike to be brothers . . . only one wore a beard and the other was clean-shaven.

After a few minutes one got up and went outside while the other remained seated. Right then was when I knew for sure they planned more than just looking.

Sure enough, after another ten minutes those miners finished their drinks, pocketed their money, and left. The thug sitting at the table waited thirty seconds, then followed them outside.

Being the knothead I am, I waited another thirty seconds and followed the thug.

It was near midnight and bitter cold. A light snow was falling and the wind was whipping it across the street in white rivulets. If there was a moon it was covered by clouds, and it was too dark to see much more than ten feet or so down the street.

The miners were far enough ahead to be out of sight, but I could hear the sound of their boots and the soft murmur of their voices. Now and then one of them laughed, and that carried loud and plain.

The thug I was following was only a dim outline in the night. The miners' bootsteps stopped, and one of the miners swore loudly. The thug kept walking until he was right behind them, then pulled his pistol. The sound of it cocking was uncommonly sharp in the sudden quiet.

"You're covered on both sides," he said to the miners. "Just do like you're told and all you'll lose is your money."

I was still a ways back, but I moved up slow and easy, wanting to get as close to the nearest thug as possible. When I was five feet away one of the miners saw me. There was no telling how well he could see me, but I pointed toward the far side of him and mouthed that he should distract the other thug.

Now, all I could see of the miner was a vague, dim form in the darkness, but his eyes must have been a lot better than mine because he caught my meaning right away. He started cussing a blue streak, letting the words out loud enough to shock the devil himself.

I slipped my Colt from the holster and slammed it down hard right behind the nearest thug's ear. I caught him so he wouldn't make too much noise as he fell.

"Damn it," the other thug said to the cussing miner. "If you don't shut up I'll put a bullet in you right now. Just shut up and start moving down that alley. And remember, my partner is right behind you."

That miner looked toward me again and I nodded. He led the way into the alley. As they walked down the alley I moved behind them, putting myself closer to the second thief. He thought I was his partner and paid no attention to me until I was right beside him.

Then he squinted at me, and even in the darkness I saw his eyes go wide and his mouth gape in puzzlement. But my Colt was within an inch of his nose before he could react, and when I thumbed back the hammer he swallowed hard.

One of the miners took his gun, and all that remained was walking him, and dragging his still unconscious friend, to the sheriff's office. The sheriff was asleep on a cot in the back of the jail, but when we showed him our prizes he perked right up.

"Been trying to catch this pair red-handed for two months," he said. "Guess their luck finally ran out."

Turned out they were brothers. Twins, in fact. Samuel and Joshua Clemens. They hailed from Ohio, and while they were only thirty-three, both had served time on more than one occasion.

Samuel was the one I'd clipped on the back of the head. He came to right after we reached the sheriff's office, and sat bent over in the cell, moaning and rubbing the back of his head. Joshua Clemens was the one with the beard, and he gave me a hard look. "They can't keep us locked up forever," he said. "When we get out I'm going to kill you."

I didn't pay him any mind—I'd heard hard talk before. No point losing any sleep over it.

Turned out the four miners also were related. Two of them, Thomas and Henry Walsh, were brothers. Thomas was the younger, just twenty-one, short but strongly built. He had a baby face and a sheepish grin. Henry was a year shy of thirty; he was tall, dark, and rangy.

Raymond Walsh was their uncle, but scarcely older than Henry. He had a pleasant manner and laughed at the drop of a joke. It was he who took the meaning of my words back at the robbery and let out the cussing streak.

Owen Newberry was a cousin, and like the others he was fairly young. He sported a mustache and a beard along the line of his jaw, and of the four, he seemed to have been around the most. He kept looking at me with a strange expression on his face until I gave my name.

Then he smiled and chuckled. "I knew it," he said. "I couldn't put my finger on where and when, but I knew I'd seen you somewhere.

"The rest of the folks here are from California, but I'm Texas born and New Mexico bred. That's where I saw you, in New Mexico. About four, five years back, I think.

"My pa owned a small ranch near the Colorado border, and that year I helped take a small herd into Alamitos. There was quite a stir going on at the time, and you were right at the heart of it. You were marshal or sheriff, right? Before it was over, most of the rustlers were either dead or in jail. Seems to me you were set to marry some real pretty little lady when I had to leave?"

"I did. Marrying Mary Kay was the best thing that ever happened to me."

"Never been married myself," Owen said. "Might be I'm

just a shade too good at ducking ropes. Henry there has a wife and four kids back in California. He'll talk your ear off about 'em if you give him half a chance."

We left the sheriff's office and went our separate ways, but not before each of them said thanks about twenty times.

Three days later the army gave up trying to keep the miners out of the Black Hills, and the stampede was on for real. Trouble was, I was still hustling work and no closer to getting an outfit together than the day I arrived.

Then a gent wearing a real nice suit showed up at the livery one evening as I was about to bed down. He was driving a wagon, and that wagon was loaded to the rafters with gear. He climbed down from the wagon and yelled out my name, so I came down to see what the fuss was all about.

He asked if I was James Darnell and I said yes. He pulled a small ledger book from his pocket and had me write my name, then asked if I needed help unloading the wagon.

"Why would I want to unload the wagon at all?" I asked. "And while we're at it, why did I just write my name in that book of yours?"

That fellow looked at me like I was dense, which I often am. "You signed the book to show I made delivery," he said. "You want to unload the wagon because all that stuff in it is yours, but the wagon is mine.

"If you look down the street there, you'll see a sign that says 'Dobbs' Mercantile.' I'm the Dobbs in the sign. Normally I don't make deliveries, but the folks who paid for this stuff made me promise to turn it over to you personal. So here it is."

"Folks? What folks?"

"I don't remember their names, except for the one called Newberry. But they bought all this stuff and a lot more, so I figured the least I could do was see you got it. Now do you need help unloading it or not?"

Well, I still didn't know what to make of it, but I took to unloading the wagon and had everything on the ground in a few minutes. Most of it was boxed or wrapped, so I still wasn't sure what all I had, but there was plenty of it.

That Mr. Dobbs started to climb into the wagon, then reached into his coat pocket and took out an envelope.

"Almost forgot about this," he said. "Maybe it will give you some answers."

He drove the wagon back the way he came and I opened the envelope. Inside was near two hundred dollars in cash, along with a note.

We heard you wasn't having much luck putting an outfit together. We also figured you'd say no if we tried to give you money, so we bought this stuff and took off for gold country.

A fellow told us of a rich strike in a place called Deadwood Gulch. It's more to the north, but sounds good. If you come that way, look us up. We still owe you plenty.

The note was signed "Owen Newberry." I read it twice, then stood there flabbergasted.

Then I got busy opening boxes and unwrapping things. Pretty soon it was all out in the open where I could see it, and all I could do was shake my head.

It looked like Old Man Trouble had done me a good turn for a change.

CHAPTER 2

THOSE boys had bought me an outfit complete to the last detail. A quick list came up with two woolen blankets, one rubber blanket, two pair of heavy leather boots, one pair of rubber hip boots, a round-pointed shovel, a pick, a gold pan, two tin plates, a frying pan, a dutch oven, a tin pail, two hacksaws, and a tent.

They'd also thought to include such staples as twenty pounds of sugar, seventy-five pounds of flour, three pounds of baking soda, and fifty pounds of beans.

It was as complete an outfit as I could imagine, and far better than any I'd expected to put together for myself. About the only thing missing was a couple of pack mules, and maybe some spare ammunition, but I allowed that was what the money was for and spent it accordingly.

The leather boots were a couple of sizes too small, but I took them back to the mercantile next morning and traded them for two other pair that fit proper. I owned a nearly new Winchester rifle and a Colt pistol that used the same .44-caliber ammunition, so I bought two hundred rounds of .44s in case somebody started a war and invited me along.

Then I spent most of the day trying to find a couple of mules at an affordable price. Not long before dark I bought my first mule from a miner who'd already been to the Black Hills and decided he wasn't cut out for the life. The second mule I bought wasn't as young, as strong, or as big as the first, but cost me twenty dollars more.

As an afterthought, I bought fifty rounds of ammunition for the Colt revolving shotgun I keep in a scabbard on my saddle. One thing I'd learned long ago—a 12-gauge loaded with buckshot can come in mighty handy. I also bought twenty pounds of coffee beans, knowing it would be a long, cold winter in the Black Hills.

It would have been nice to add a stove to my equipment, but just the thought of hauling one all that way was enough to make my back hurt.

Besides, I knew enough about northern winters to not even consider living in a tent, though it could be done. First thing I'd do after staking my claim would be to build a cabin. A cabin with a big fireplace.

Now, I'm decent with a rope and better than fair with a gun. Put me into any kind of a tussle and I'll hold my own. But sit me down with a pen and piece of paper, tell me to write a letter, and I'm near helpless. Yet it didn't seem proper to ride off into the Black Hills without sending Mary Kay a letter, so I sat down and scratched one out.

Scratched is right. When I was finished, it looked like a drunken chicken had stepped in ink, then staggered all over a perfectly good piece of paper. But there at the end I wrote "I love you" in big, bold letters, and signed my name plain. When it came right down to it, that was all I wanted to get across anyway.

I posted the letter, and just as it started to grow light the next morning, I ate a good breakfast, saddled Cap, and loaded the mules. Then we left Cheyenne and pointed toward the Black Hills.

It was a bit below freezing, and a cold north wind was whipping snow around like frozen needles. But we were on the trail again, headed for wild country, and that's a mighty fine feeling. Cap was stepping right along, his breath coming out like white geysers. Seemed as if he liked that country as much as I did.

Five miles outside of Cheyenne I saw a line of black shapes bobbing in the distance. As they came closer I realized it was a cavalry troop. I angled Cap to intercept them, thinking to pick up news of the trail and of any Sioux activity in the area.

Turned out they were wearing buffalo robes, and that's why they looked black from a distance. A Lieutenant Masterson was in charge, and he was mighty surprised to come across a lone white man headed into the heart of Sioux country. He told me I should turn back. "Get at least three or four men to ride with," he said. "Ten or twelve would be even better. A single white man hauling all that gear is ripe fruit to a Sioux war party."

"Lieutenant," I said, "I been riding wild country since I was knee-high to a tall grasshopper. In the first place, most Indians won't go galavanting around in this weather unless they have to. For the most part, they've laid in food for the winter, and they have plenty of buffalo hides to keep them warm. Think on it—if you had the choice of snuggling down in a warm teepee with plenty of food and a young squaw by your side, or riding around in this weather looking for someone to scalp, which would you do?"

He laughed. "No wonder we haven't seen hide nor hair of any Sioux. You can't count on anything, though. Come spring, this country won't be safe for any of us. But if you want to risk losing your scalp, I won't try to stop you."

We talked for a few minutes about trail conditions and the like, then the cold wind got the better of us and we each went on our way. But in spite of what I told Lieutenant Masterson, I rode almighty careful. It was true enough that no Indian liked being out in such weather, but all it took was one Sioux brave to have a spat with his woman and come riding my way to cool off. I stuck to rough country and kept my eyes open.

For the first five or six days on the trail about all I did was shiver and shake, and the sound of my teeth chattering was loud enough to wake a hibernating grizzly. Then my body seemed to adapt to the cold, and after that it rarely bothered me. Cap had his winter coat of hair, and he paid no mind at all to the cold.

The two mules had as much hair as Cap, but they were so

dang cantankerous that before long I was almost hoping they would freeze to death.

From Cheyenne to Deadwood Gulch in Dakota Territory is one hell of a ride even in good weather, but I pointed Cap northeast, thinking to strike the Belle Fourche River and follow that to Whitewood Creek. Whitewood Creek, in turn, was supposed to take me to Deadwood Gulch.

It was a ride of better than six hundred miles, and I figured to make twenty miles a day. That worked out to exactly a month on the trail, and in the winter, that's a long, weary time.

But me and Cap took it easy, and the first week went about as smooth as you could expect when your only company is a pair of mules. The second day out one of those mules came up and nipped Cap's tail with his teeth. Cap lashed out with his back hooves and knocked the mule flat.

Fortunately, none of the gear was damaged, and the mule, though it limped for a few miles, wasn't seriously hurt either. But it never tried to bite Cap again.

Then, on the seventh or eighth day out, it began to snow harder than before. Big, wet flakes that built quickly on the ground. The wind started blowing like a banshee from hell, and the snow fell even faster. We found ourselves in the heart of a blizzard.

The temperature dropped, and soon the land was buried totally under snow. Me, I couldn't see a thing, and Cap wasn't doing much better. Going north as we were, that blizzard was hitting us right in the face.

Travel became impossible, so we looked for a place to fort up until the storm broke. What we found was just a nook in the rocks away from the wind and blowing snow, but I chopped down half a dozen small pine trees and used them to wall us in.

There was just enough room back in the nook for the mules, Cap, and myself, but once I had a fire going it was at least livable. Not comfortable, maybe, but it would do until the blizzard stopped.

Way I had it figured, there were likely miners all over the trails. Owen Newberry and his friends couldn't be more than a couple of days ahead of me themselves, and I imagined hundreds of others were scattered about here and there, all headed for some part of the Black Hills.

As usual, I'd chosen the roughest trails and the lonesomest country to travel through, so it might be that miles and miles were between me and the nearest white man, but it was still a comfort to know that others had been caught by the same storm. Misery really does love company.

The blizzard raged and howled for the better part of three days, then, along about noon of the third day, it simply stopped. One minute the wind was howling, the snow was falling, and I was beginning to talk to myself. The next minute the wind stopped and blue sky showed through the layer of dark clouds.

When that patch of blue showed itself I knew the blizzard was over, and I started digging us out. There was no more than three feet of snow on the level, but the wind had piled it into drifts more than twelve feet high in places. The trees somehow managed to keep their burdens of snow in spite of the wind, and when the sun came out and struck the glistening landscape, it was blinding and beautiful.

The days are short in that northern country, and it seemed best to wait for morning before starting up the trail again, but I packed everything that wasn't essential so we would be ready for an early start. Cap was a large horse and wouldn't have much trouble with the snow, but the mules were stubborn, and I'd no idea how they would react.

Along about dark I ate a plate of beans and drank half a pot of coffee, then settled in for the night. It was still cold, but not as bad as before, and the thick blankets along with a fire soon had me warm enough to sleep.

But just as I dozed off something made my eyes snap wide

open. For a time I lay there, listening intently, wondering what had disturbed me. Had Cap or one of the mules made some unusual sound? Was an animal of some kind prowling about in the night?

The thought was strong in my mind that some sound had awakened me, but now there was nothing. Cap stomped a foot and whinnied softly . . . one of the mules broke wind . . . the fire crackled. But there was no sound that should have disturbed my sleep.

Then something like a moan drifted to my ears. It seemed to come from some distance away, but after a time I heard it again. It seemed closer.

Slipping from my blankets, I quietly got dressed, putting on my gun belt first, then my hat, boots, and coat. I had gloves, but that was wild country and it might be I'd have to use my gun. The gloves stayed where they were.

My fire was small, and concealed as it was by the rocks and the trees I'd cut, I doubted it could be seen from more than thirty yards; but that was still taking too much of a chance. I carefully smothered the fire with snow, then eased out of the shelter and into the open.

The moon was high and bright and I could see well. Too well, almost. Yet for a time I saw nothing. Moving around the rocks, I looked across a treeless meadow that stretched a quarter mile to the east.

There, no more than seventy yards from where I stood, something dark moved against the white background of the snow. For a minute I thought it was a wolf. Then it stood up and staggered forward. What I took for a wolf was obviously a person.

For a minute I was too surprised to react. There was no good reason I could think of to explain why a lone person should be trying to walk through three feet of snow in a high meadow on a cold November night.

The person fell face forward, slowly stood up, and started walking again. He fell a second time and remained down.

Me, I figured some unfortunate soul was in a world of trouble out there, but I wasn't about to go running into the meadow to see if I might help.

First thing I did was take my eyes off the person in the snow. I spent the next five minutes studying the surrounding country inch by inch, looking for any movement, any shape that didn't seem natural. There was nothing.

Only then did I move slowly toward the shape in the snow. My rifle was in my hands and a round was in the chamber. When I was close enough to see better, I realized the person was an Indian. He'd fallen in a tight bundle, but I could see his hands and they were empty.

Very carefully, I rolled him over . . . only it wasn't a him. She was an Indian girl, no more than thirteen or fourteen by the looks of her. She wore only a buckskin dress and a pair of moccasins. Her wrist had a strong, steady pulse, but she was cold. Too cold.

Even soaking wet as she was, she couldn't have weighed more than a hundred and ten pounds, so I just scooped her up onto my shoulder and walked back to my shelter in the rocks.

Easing her gently onto my blankets, I quickly rebuilt the fire and put coffee on. When it was going good I examined the girl. She was bruised and scraped, but didn't seem to be seriously hurt.

After some hesitation, I stripped off her dress and moccasins, covering her with a blanket. She was still unconscious, but I was able to get several sips of hot coffee down her throat. Then, when she would take no more coffee, I sat back and watched her, not knowing what else to do.

Twenty minutes later she began to stir, and her eyes fluttered open. For a few moments she looked around calmly, likely trying to figure out where she was. Then her eyes focused on me. The reaction was instantaneous.

She screamed and left the blankets like a shot, but she chose the wrong direction to run and ended up huddled against the cold, bare face of the rock outcropping behind her. Her eyes darted this way and that, searching for a way of escape, and those eyes were filled with terror.

I opened my hands and held them toward her, palms out. "I won't hurt you," I said. "I found you in the snow. Can you speak English?"

For the space of ten seconds she just looked at me, then, realizing she was naked, she sank to the ground and drew her knees up to her chest. "My father was white," she said. "I understand."

Slowly, I picked up a blanket and tossed it to her. She caught it and wrapped it around herself. Now that she was awake I realized she was some older than I'd first thought, but still likely shy of eighteen.

"Who are you?" I asked. "Why were you out here all alone?"

She decided to trust me. In surprisingly good English she quickly told her story. Her name was Eyes-Like-Water, and it fit. For the first time I saw that her eyes were blue. She said that she and her mate were traveling to a larger encampment when the blizzard caught them. When it broke they started traveling again immediately, but as evening came they blundered into a camp where four white men had been waiting out the storm.

Without warning, one of the white men shot her mate, then they dragged her off her horse and started to tear at her clothing. But her man wasn't dead, and he managed to distract them by putting a rifle bullet into the one nearest him. That was the chance she needed and she took off running. She didn't look back until she was several hundred yards away.

"I think Black Eagle was badly hurt," she said, "but I'm sure he got away. I must find him."

"Where would he go if he did get away?" I asked. "Is there some way I could find him?'

She thought for a couple of minutes. "There is a place,"

she said. "A cave, two miles there." She pointed to the north. "He would go to it if he had the strength."

I asked exactly where we were and she told me. The answer surprised me a little. I'd wanted to make twenty miles a day, and thought that was slow, but according to her I was no more than seventy-five miles from Cheyenne and the river I'd crossed the day before the blizzard was the North Platte.

We were no more than a skip and a holler from Fort Laramie, but Eyes-Like-Water said they seldom if ever sent out patrols in such weather. That's one of the reasons she and Black Eagle chose this time to travel.

Whoever shot Black Eagle without warning and tried to rape Eyes-Like-Water was a no-good bastard. Way I look at it, a person is a person regardless of the color of their skin. If a man takes a swing at me, I'll do my best to knock some sense into him, whoever he is. If he takes a shot at me, I'll shoot back as quick and straight as I can.

But if a man treats me with respect, I'll do the same for him no matter what color he is.

Some might have said this was none of my business, but to me, helping someone in need was every man's business. I'd brought Eyes-Like-Water into my camp, and you could say I'd taken responsibility for her and for her trouble, when I did that.

"You were walking north when I found you," I said. "Is that where you were headed?"

"No. I was just running. I hadn't thought about the cave until you asked."

"Tell me how to find the cave. If Black Eagle is there I'll bring him back."

She shook her head. "He would try to kill you unless I'm with you."

Now, the last thing on earth I wanted to do was go riding through that country at night in search of a wounded Dakota Sioux. And having an Indian girl along didn't make it one bit more appealing, even if she was cute as a button.

It was my turn to do some thinking. "Would the cave make a good camp?" I asked. "I mean, for me and my things? Two mules and a horse take up a lot of room."

"The cave is large enough. There is even a tunnel where someone made a room by building walls. Horses can be kept there."

"Then let's see if Black Eagle made it that far," I said. "It won't take me long to get ready."

Her dress would take hours to dry, but I had spare things and I gave them to her. I'd a new pair of long johns, and she climbed into them, rolling the sleeves and legs up. She put a flannel shirt on over that and pulled two pairs of socks onto her feet.

With a blanket wrapped around her, I figured she would stay warm enough.

Then, feeling like seven kinds of a fool and wondering how in hell Old Man Trouble found me seventy-five miles north of nowhere, I packed the mules, saddled Cap, and left. Eyes-Like-Water was behind me in the saddle, her arms around my waist, and as we rode into the cold, dark night I wondered what she was thinking. Most of all, I wondered if she really trusted me. I finally decided it didn't really matter. On that night I was all the hope she had.

CHAPTER 3

IT took nearly three hours to find the cave. When we did, Eyes-Like-Water went in first, using a candle from my saddlebags for light. She was inside the cave no more than thirty seconds when I heard her scream.

Leaving Cap right where he was, I went into the cave on the run, pistol out and hammer thumbed back. In the dim light of the candle I saw Eyes-Like-Water kneeling beside Black Eagle.

With a hasty fire built and the animals tucked away in the room Eyes-Like-Water showed me, I examined Black Eagle. He had three bullet wounds, and while none were serious, he'd lost more blood than a body can afford.

One bullet had entered his thigh and was still inside. A second bullet cut a deep groove along his ribs, and the third sliced the thick muscle where his neck and shoulder joined.

Like I said, none of the wounds were terribly serious, but the loss of blood could be deadly. Hell, the cold and exposure already should have killed him. How he'd made it this far amazed me.

About all you can do to treat loss of blood is to stop the bleeding, get plenty of water into the person, keep him warm, and wait. I didn't think Black Eagle had much chance, to tell the truth. But if he'd managed to reach the cave with three bullet wounds in his body, and all the way having to fight the cold and snow, maybe he could go all the way.

So I cleaned and bandaged his wounds, got some water down his throat, and bundled him in blankets. Then I tried to get some sleep while Eyes-Like-Water tended him.

I'm about as trusting as the next man, but I've got to

admit, sleep didn't come easy that night. I kept wondering what would happen if Black Eagle regained consciousness and found a white man sleeping only a few feet away.

I was up and about before the sun rose. I needn't have worried about Black Eagle. When I woke up I found him conscious, but he was about as weak and haggard looking as a man can be.

Eyes-Like-Water must have explained the situation to him, because he hadn't tried to kill me. But there was no friendliness in his eyes when they met mine. He spoke a bit of English, but not nearly as well as Eyes-Like-Water.

"Why you help?" he whispered.

I shrugged. "Seemed like the thing to do," I said.

He said nothing else and I slipped into my coat and walked outside to gather some firewood and take care of my morning chores. When I came back in, Black Eagle was already looking stronger and Eyes-Like-Water had coffee going over the fire.

That's the thing about losing blood—it can kill you quick, but you can recover from it almost as fast. Black Eagle would be weak for a while, but unless his wounds got infected, he was in no more danger.

Me, I was in a pickle about what to do. Deadwood Gulch was getting no closer, but I couldn't just ride off and leave them. Somehow I had to get them back to their people, but it would be days before Black Eagle could sit a horse. The thought occurred to me that I might rig a travois to carry him on, but that could wait until later in the day. Then we would see.

I put it off too long. About three hours later I was sitting just inside the entrance of the cave, looking out over the country and daydreaming, when I saw the four riders coming our way.

They were white men, and they were obviously following sign in the snow. I swore softly.

I called Eyes-Like-Water, and she took one look at them

before confirming my fears. It was the same four men who'd shot Black Eagle. They kept coming, and then they spotted the cave. For a few minutes they sat in the saddle and talked among themselves, then they started forward. They must have known Black Eagle had lost his rifle, or they wouldn't have come straight in like that.

Now, the area outside the cave was littered with boulders and rock outcroppings for two hundred yards in every direction, and that offered good shelter to anyone out there. But the cave entrance was a bit higher than the surrounding country, giving us a small advantage.

Behind me, the rock turned into a middling-size mountain, and it was that mountain the cave sank into. About the only advantage to that was those men couldn't circle us and come in from behind. If they wanted us, they had to come in and get us. But the sad truth was, there was far more cover outside the cave than inside, so when those men hit the twenty-five-yard mark I stepped outside to meet them, my Winchester in my right hand.

I didn't point it at them, but held it aimed at the ground, my hand wrapped around the action, my thumb on the hammer. They saw me at once and it took them by surprise. They'd been trailing an Indian, or so they thought, and now here I was. They reined in four abreast. It was then I noticed one of them had his leg heavily bandaged. A trace of blood showed through the dirty cloth used to wrap the leg, and I figured that was the man Black Eagle had shot. It was a shame he hadn't shot two feet higher and a little to the right.

"Something I can do for you boys?" I asked.

It didn't take them long to get over their surprise.

"We trailed an Injun here," one of them said. "We put a couple of bullets in him yesterday, but he slipped away. Had a real pretty squaw with him, too. Don't suppose you've seen either of 'em?"

All four of them wore buffalo robes and felt hats. Two had full beards, one had a thick mustache, and the last was clean-shaven except for a day's stubble. All four carried heavy rifles across their saddles.

"They're in the cave," I said. "But you can't have them."

The four looked at me like I was crazy. "Hell," one of them said. "The buck's as good as dead already, and that squaw can handle five as well as four. No need to get selfish about it. Why don't we all just go into the cave and I'll show you what I mean?"

It was cold out there with the wind whipping around and finding weaknesses in my coat. But a deeper cold was growing inside me. Those four weren't going to ride off and forget Eyes-Like-Water, and I wasn't going to move and let them have her. That left few choices.

"There's been enough talk," I said. "She's inside, you're outside, and that's how it's going to stay."

"That your last word?" Mustache asked.

I said nothing and he spat in the snow. "Damn," he said. "I wish there was another way, but—"

He suddenly jerked his rifle off the saddle and swung the barrel in my direction. I'd been waiting for that move since they rode up, so I tilted my Winchester up, cocking the hammer as it came in line, and fired from the hip. The bullet caught Mustache in the belly and slammed him backward off his horse.

He screamed, but I was already diving for cover. A bullet pinged off a rock near my head, and two others whistled through the air, sounding too close. I hit, rolled over twice, and came up behind a boulder. When I brought my rifle out for a shot the three men still in the saddle were skedaddling back the way they'd come.

I might have taken a second man out, but I didn't like the thought of shooting a man in the back . . . even if he deserved it.

They pulled in behind some boulders about five hundred yards away, then the shooting started for real. Trouble was, those men had .50-caliber buffalo rifles, Sharps by the look and sound of them, and all I had was a .44-caliber Winchester.

Now, a Winchester is a fine rifle, and the .44 is a decent cartridge. It's real handy to need only one kind of ammunition that will fit both rifle and pistol, but there's also a big drawback in it, and right then I was facing that drawback. A .44 just isn't all that powerful a cartridge, even in a rifle.

I could reach those men with a bullet, but the rainbow trajectory of the .44 made hitting anything at five hundred yards mighty tough. On the other hand, five hundred yards was right next door for those big .50s.

So for the next ten minutes I wasted a lot of bullets, and they came close to parting my hair with every shot. It looked bad all around.

The man I'd shot out of the saddle was on all fours now, moaning in pain. But he wasn't through trying. With blood all over him, he crawled to his rifle, picked it up, and came to his knees for a shot at me.

I shot him twice more, both bullets taking him in the chest and putting him down for keeps.

After a time the shooting slowed and I used all the cover I could find to get back to the cave. The last twenty feet or so there was no cover, and I crossed that gap in a sudden spring that must have taken those men by surprise.

Leastways, I was already inside the cave before they got off a shot.

But then they did the thing I feared the most: they began firing randomly into the cave. Bullets slammed off the rock walls, sometimes ricocheting several times before sailing away down the tunnel.

Black Eagle and Eyes-Like-Water were a lot smarter than I was and suggested we move into the room occupied by the animals. We moved quickly, Eyes-Like-Water leading the way, and me carrying Black Eagle.

Strictly speaking, it wasn't really a room at all. It was a branch of the main tunnel, but someone had brought rocks in and walled the tunnel up from floor to ceiling about forty feet from the opening. Then they walled up the opening, leaving only enough room for a good-sized door.

The door itself was made of thick saplings, and with that closed we were reasonably safe from ricocheting bullets. But we couldn't stay there forever. Sooner or later they would begin to wonder why I wasn't returning their fire. When that happened they would come looking, and if they caught us in the room we were in serious trouble.

I hoped they would wait until night. Then I just might be able to sneak out there and teach them something about shooting at a more reasonable range.

Black Eagle was still weak as a kitten, but he was trying to sit up, and I decided it couldn't hurt him. I helped him get his back against the wall, and while he wasn't about to go dancing for a spell, he looked strong enough to hold a gun.

I still had that Colt revolving shotgun, and there was a spare pistol tucked into my saddlebags. The shotgun I gave to Black Eagle, and the pistol to Eyes-Like-Water. Black Eagle's eyes glinted as he accepted the shotgun.

"How you know I not kill you?" he asked.

"Will you?"

For a time he just looked at me, the glint still in his eyes. Then he came as close to smiling as I've ever seen a man do without moving his mouth. "No," he said.

The firing from outside stopped, so I opened the door and eased out. There was no more firing, so I built a fire near the entrance to the room and fixed enough food to feed all three of us. We ate in silence.

By noon the silence had me worried. Were the men still out there? Were they even now circling around and coming at us from both sides? There was no way of knowing, and that worried me.

I could see no sign of them from the cave entrance, but just to be on the safe side, I saddled Cap and stripped the mules of gear. If we had to make a break, I wanted to be ready.

Then the rifle fire started again, much closer and from both sides, pinning us in. We ducked into the room and closed the door, leaving just enough of a crack to see out. Even as I watched, brush started falling right in front of the cave, being tossed from both sides. Those men were still out there, all right, and they were building our funeral pyre.

Shoving the door open, I ran to the cave mouth, hoping to stop them from lighting the fire. But even as I neared the opening a bullet burned across my shoulder and a torch fell onto the brush.

I dropped to the rock floor as other bullets slashed past me. The brush burst into flame and more brush was tossed onto the pile. Thick smoke poured into the cave.

Horseshoes on stone sounded behind me, then Cap went past and out the opening of the cave at a gallop. Eyes-Like-Water was on Cap's back and hunched low in the saddle. It was the last thing those men out there expected.

It must have been a shock when Cap burst suddenly through the smoke and fire. It must have frozen them for a second or two as well, because by the time someone fired at Cap he was already fifty yards away and running like a scalded hound.

Taking the opportunity, I ran to the mouth of the cave, coughing and almost blinded by the smoke. I couldn't see a thing, but I emptied my rifle in both directions, hoping to distract the men long enough to let Cap and Eyes-Like-Water get away. It must have worked, because through a wind-whipped gap in the smoke I saw Cap reach the shelter of a rock outcropping and disappear behind it.

But then he reappeared on the other side, still running strong. Two shots rang out and Cap seemed to flinch, but kept running. Then he was out of range and all three men turned their full attention back to me. But I was already heading back into the room, bullets chewing up the rock all around me. Luck was with me, and I made it unharmed.

I shut the door behind me, but knew the smoke would make its way through sooner or later.

"Where is she?" I asked Black Eagle. "Where did Eyes-Like-Water go?"

"She go for help. Three hour, more than three hour, she come back."

In three hours, I thought, we'll probably both be dead. But maybe those bastards out there would wait around long enough to run into a few dozen Sioux warriors. That was something.

The door did a better job than I thought it would in keeping the smoke out. But after a time it began to come in, the air grew thick, and we began to cough.

Staying low, I moved to the rear wall, thinking to go through it to the tunnel beyond, but whoever built that wall did it right. None of the rocks weighed less than a couple of hundred pounds, and they were mortared together.

By the light of a candle, I managed to knock a large rock out of the wall at knee level. That was all I could manage to dislodge, and the smoke was getting thicker by the second. Then I remembered my mining equipment. Quickly locating the pick, I went at the wall like a madman.

In a few minutes I had a three-foot-wide opening broken through the wall. But when I stuck my head and shoulders into the opening and gasped for air, the darkness seemed strangely larger and colder than it should have.

I held a candle through the opening. I saw nothing. The darkness swallowed the light of the candle as though it didn't exist. I saw no hint of floor, ceiling, or walls. There was only endless darkness.

Shielding my eyes from the light of the candle with my hand, my eyes slowly adjusted to the darkness. Only then was I able to see distant shapes. The ceiling was fifty feet or more above me, the walls an equal distance on either side. There seemed to be no far wall, and only five feet beyond the wall was a drop-off that looked bottomless.

I tossed a piece of broken rock over the drop-off. It fell for a long, long time before it rattled off stone, fell again, then splashed into water. We were trapped. There was no way on God's green earth to get past that chasm.

Opening the hole in the wall did allow the smoke to be sucked out of the room, however, or at least enough of it to let us breathe.

CHAPTER 4

THE mules had been close to panicking, though contrary as a mule is, he won't panic anywhere near as fast as a horse. With much of the smoke drawn out through the wall they calmed down, so it looked like we wouldn't suffocate and we wouldn't be trampled by scared mules. That didn't mean our troubles were over.

An hour passed, then part of another. Just over two hours after the fire started, those men came looking for our bodies.

The smoke had cleared, but I was slow in noticing it and heard no one coming until they were already inside the cave. They would have seen the walled-up room right away, of course, and it was an easy guess to think we were inside.

I heard their voices through the thick door, only by then it was too late to stop them. They used some choice language, taunting us and the like. They had us and they knew it. The door was thick enough to stop a bullet, and they didn't even try to break it down

Instead, they repeated their fire trick, stacking wood against the base of the door and lighting it. That door was old and dry. In seconds it was aflame. Before long the fire spurted through our side of the door, and then they all started shooting with those damn .50 calibers.

Weakened as it was by the fire, the door never even slowed the bullets down. A mule took a bullet through the head and barely had time to kick before dying. The second mule took two bullets in the gut and died harder, but it died just the same.

The safest place for me and Black Eagle was against the wall where the door was. But the fire made the stone in that wall hot enough to burn a man. I pulled Black Eagle behind one of the dead mules and dropped behind the other myself.

I put three bullets through my side of the door, which startled the men outside for just a minute. Then they started shooting again, the bullets searching the room in hunt of a target.

A bullet hit the rock on the far side of my head and spattered my face with razor-sharp fragments. A second bullet struck rock right between my legs, but somehow bounced away without doing damage.

Then the burning door collapsed. For a moment I saw nothing, then a man wearing a buffalo robe coat was silhouetted in the opening. His rifle was aimed right at me, and his finger was on the trigger. I tried desperately to bring my rifle around, knowing all the while I was going to be too late.

Only he didn't shoot. A surprised look suddenly flashed across his face, and he fell face down. Three arrows were sticking out of his back. Savage yells filled the air, several shots rang out, then there was silence.

A moment later Eyes-Like-Water stood in the doorway. There was still a good bit of fire and hot coals lying about, but she picked her way through it and went to Black Eagle. Three brawny Sioux followed her in, and they carried Black Eagle outside. I climbed wearily to my feet and followed them.

Forty or more Sioux warriors milled about outside the cave, and I don't remember any of them except Eyes-Like-Water looking at me kindly, but none of them tried to shoot me either. I took that for a good sign.

Eyes-Like-Water told me it was Cap who saved us. He'd gone through the snow almost like it wasn't there, and she'd reached her people sooner than she thought possible.

Those Sioux may not have looked all that friendly, but when they rode away I had four fine ponies to replace my dead mules. One mighty impressive-looking Sioux spoke to me for a minute before they left, and Eyes-Like-Water translated what he said.

Seems his people were going to move up near the Little Bighorn come spring. I was always welcome in any Sioux camp, he said, and he would be honored if I would visit them when the sun again warmed the land.

I thanked him as best I could and promised to come to their camp if it were possible. It turned out they were Oglala Sioux, and they had the reputation of being the best fighters of all the plains tribes. Just before they left, Eyes-Like-Water told me the name of the Sioux who thanked me. His name was Sitting Bull. He was an old man, no longer an active warrior, but still a major leader among the Sioux. I knew the name, as did every white man west of the Mississippi.

I can't remember ever being overly impressed at the mention of a man's name, but that one shook me a little.

And I was awfully glad I was on the right side in this fight. Inside the cave lay the bodies of the men who only minutes before had been trying to kill us. Now they were riddled with arrows and bullets. All were missing their hair, and a few other parts as well.

I had a nasty cut on my shoulder from a bullet, several burns, and a good-sized bump on my head that I couldn't remember getting. That bump was above my left eye, and it was near as big as a hen's egg.

Once I noticed the bump it started hurting like hell, but I didn't care. It would have been all too easy for me to be lying there on the ground, dead as the others, so I just bandaged my shoulder, rubbed a little grease on my burns, and counted myself lucky.

Then I ate a bit, drank some coffee, packed my gear onto those Indian ponies, and started again for Deadwood Gulch. From that point on I rode with even more caution, praying the remainder of the trip would be uneventful. It was.

CHAPTER 5

ALMOST a month later to the day, I came to the Belle Fourche, followed that to Whitewood Creek, and followed that to Deadwood Gulch. It wasn't much to look at, but you could almost smell the gold.

Deadwood Gulch lies in the valley of Whitewood Creek, and hills rise up six or seven hundred feet on both sides. Most folks there referred to those hills as mountains, but we had gophers in Colorado that could do better than that.

Yet there was no denying it was lovely country. The Black Hills were so named because of the dark green trees covering the hills—from a distance the trees look black.

There were miners in Deadwood Gulch when I arrived, but not many. No more than fifty on the highest count. That meant a man could still claim land along Whitewood Creek, and as soon as my tent was pitched and my gear stowed away, I set about doing exactly that.

Now, a claim in Deadwood Gulch was a mighty generous thing. It ran three hundred feet up and down the creek, and from rimrock to rimrock on either side. That's a lot of land any way you look at it. My first claim was staked right along the creek, but I had something more in mind.

Thing was, I knew more about hardrock mining than about placer gold, so I staked another claim up a side gorge from Whitewood Creek. It was higher ground, and a small deposit of quartz showed enough color to make starting a shaft there look like a good idea.

And just as importantly, it was the perfect spot to build a cabin. Most of the miners were living right along the creek, and I counted at least twenty tents and half a dozen small cabins. Several other cabins were under construction, again along the creek, and all I could do was shake my head.

Might have been I was overly cautious, but it looked to me like a dangerous place to live. Whitewood Creek was small, but you could see where past floods had rushed through the valley, and the high-water mark was an amazing distance from where the water now flowed. If one of those floods came along, there would be an awful bunch of men trying to hold their cabins in place with one hand while treading water with the other.

Besides, I'm a man who likes his privacy, and it wasn't likely too many men would be looking to build back where I chose. Not with all that tempting land down along the creek.

I hadn't been in camp much over an hour when Owen Newberry spotted me and let out a yell. He asked me over to his claim and I went willingly. He and his relatives had staked adjoining sections, and when I came walking up with Owen they all came over to say hello.

They had two tents up, both with stoves, though how they packed them in was beyond me. We went into one of the tents and Henry Walsh broke out a bottle of whiskey. Not caring much for the stuff, I nevertheless took the offered glass and sipped at it occasionally as we talked of Deadwood Gulch.

It was below freezing, and with the water and gravel congealed with ice, nobody was doing any real placering. That would get under way with the coming of the spring thaw. But everybody was hard at work improving their claims, and trying to dig out just enough gravel to get a feel for their prospects.

Raymond Walsh swallowed a healthy mouthful of whiskey, shuddered a bit, then lit his pipe. "I think we're all going to be rich," he said. "You can't get at the gold yet, but yesterday I got out enough deep gravel to test my claim.

"First pan had near three dollars of gold dust in it, and not a pan showed less than a dollar. Might be I just hit an unusually good bit of gravel, but I don't think so. Yes sir, I think we're all gonna be rich come spring."

I didn't hear anyone trying to argue with him, and I was in no mood to do so myself. I'd been around gold a time or two, and it was pretty certain that a few here would get rich. But come spring the whole area would be overrun with miners. Thousands of them.

They would come from everywhere. The young, the old, the wise, and the foolish. Some would get lucky, but most would be lucky to break even. For every miner who left Deadwood Gulch rich, a hundred would go home poorer than when they came.

But some few would certainly get rich, and there was no reason to believe the four of us wouldn't be among that lucky number.

All I really wanted was enough to start another ranch. If a man looked around he could still get prime cattle land just by filing on it, but a good herd of breeding cattle cost money.

Only a few years earlier a man could ride out with a rope, throw it over as many unbranded cattle as he needed, and start a ranch and build a herd with no more than a lot of backbreaking work. No longer.

Building a herd from unbranded stock—mavericking— now was likely to get a man hanged for a rustler. So I needed money if I wanted to build a ranch.

And I didn't need all that much money when compared to how much some would take out of Deadwood Gulch. Say five thousand for cattle, two or three thousand for a house and barn, and maybe a couple thousand more to keep the wolf away from the door until the herd grew large enough to start selling a few at market each year.

I did some quick figuring and came up with nine thousand dollars. Throwing in another thousand for luck, I decided that if I could coax ten thousand dollars from the gravel of Deadwood Gulch, I'd ride away a happy man.

But, hell, ten thousand dollars was rich, as far as I was

concerned. Many a time I'd punched cows for a dollar a day, and at that rate it would take something like twenty-seven years to earn ten thousand dollars. And here I was wanting to earn it in a few months.

But what choice did I have? Punching cows at a dollar a day was fine for a lone-riding man, but I had a family to support. Ten thousand dollars might be an impossible dream, but the only way I'd know would be to try.

Thomas Walsh was saying something, and I shook myself out of my thoughts long enough to listen. "Fellow I talked to this morning claimed he found a single pocket of gold that weighed in at over a thousand dollars. Just turned over one shovelful of gravel, and there she was."

"Did you actually see the gold?" Owen asked.

"No. When you get right down to it, I didn't."

For a few minutes we were all silent. Raymond tapped the ashes from his pipe and drank more whiskey. "Looks like hard weather moving in from the north," he said. "I guess we'd best get back to work."

"I guess," Tom said. "You wouldn't believe the tales I've heard of winters here. I can't say I believe all of 'em, but I'll feel better once I get a real cabin up."

"I guess you'll start building, yourself," Owen said to me. "If you need a hand, just holler."

"I'm going to build," I said, "but not here on the creek. I'll leave my tent on my claim to protect it and to give me a bit of shelter close by, but my cabin will be up yonder on my second claim."

We talked for a few minutes longer, then went about our work. But not until I made all four of them agree to let me pay them back as soon as I hit enough gold.

They were reluctant, but I wouldn't take no for an answer. They agreed more to shut me up, I think, than because they wanted to be repaid.

Owen did give me one more gift, and this one I needed. Just before I walked back to my own claim he asked if I'd thought to bring anything from Cheyenne that would hold gold dust. Being used to hardrock mining, I told him I hadn't. He gave me three sacks made from bull scrotums.

"I know it sounds strange," he said, "but it's what everybody uses. Cloth is too porous to hold fine dust, and most leather is too thick to be pliable. But take a bull scrotum and it tans into soft leather already in the shape you need.

"Don't feel bad because you didn't know about them. We didn't either until we got here. Fellow brought in a couple hundred or more and he's selling them at a dollar a shot. I bought a dozen of them myself."

Owen's expectations of Deadwood Gulch were optimistic, for him to buy so many sacks in the winter. Come spring, miners would likely bring such sacks in by the hundreds, and they'd certainly sell for less. But right then and there it was nice to have them just in case.

The rest of that first day I spent setting up my tent and making sure the boundaries of both claims were clearly marked. I also set up a makeshift corral for Cap and the ponies. It wasn't much, but it kept them out of the wind. I'd let them browse a good bit on the trail, but I took the time to gather some grass from where the wind had swept the snow away, and tossed that into the corral.

Cap wasn't in the mood to share with the ponies, so I had to go in and separate the grass into five piles so each could get a share.

It hadn't been that hard a day, to tell the truth, but by nightfall I was tuckered. I had no stove for the tent, but with the flap pointing south and a small fire built in front, it was warm enough. I wrapped up in my blankets, closed my eyes, and went to sleep. My dreams, as usual, were of Mary Kay.

Come sunrise I was already up and about. It was colder, being only a bit above zero, but there was no new snow. I made coffee, warmed more water in a pot, and washed. I'm an eating man, but first I got to get awake. That's what the coffee was for.

I wanted a bath, but there wasn't a chance. Not before spring, at least. By that time the miners coming in would find Deadwood Gulch by the smell.

I'd been wearing pointy-toed riding boots, but that morning I put on a pair of leather boots and laced them up tight. They were better suited for the work at hand, and more comfortable besides.

I ate, then sat there in front of my tent for a time, looking up toward my other claim. I was shivering in spite of the coffee, and that's what finally got me moving. Taking the axe and the pick, I walked up to the high claim.

The weather would only get worse for the next couple of months, and I needed a cabin in a hurry. What I wanted was a place large enough to live in with some comfort, a cabin with four rooms would be perfect. But that would have to wait. First I needed a much smaller place . . . just big enough to keep me out of the wind and cold.

That's the nice thing about a log cabin. You can build one any size you want, and you can build it in a number of different ways. I knew how to build two basic types, each good for a particular situation. The first cabin, the small one, would be no more than a log shack with a fireplace.

The fireplace was the ticket, and that I would build first, then add the cabin to it.

Now, I must have seen two dozen people build fireplaces over the years, and I've had a hand in building a dozen others. Near as I can recall, no two were exactly alike. But if you have good rock, and know how to make mortar, it isn't all that hard to do. In fact, I've seen a couple of fireplaces built without mortar, and they lasted for years.

I wasn't going to try that, but I didn't have to use the best mortar, or build the best fireplace either. All it had to do was hold together until spring. By that time I'd have the main cabin finished, or nearly so.

First thing I did was gather rocks—good, strong, flat rocks with no quartz showing. You get a vein of quartz in a rock, heat it, and it can explode on you. I saw a man lose an eye like that once.

When I had plenty of rocks piled up, I mixed a batch of mortar. A quick way to make decent mortar is to mix limestone dust, sand, clay, and water. The sand and limestone dust were easy, but the clay took some doing. What I needed was good, red, southern clay, but finding any at all in this frozen land was hard enough. At last I came across a spot where a small landslide had torn away a bank and exposed something that passed for clay in the north.

All that took a full day. Building the fireplace and twelve feet of chimney took two more long days, and that was pushing it. If you don't get the flue right, the fireplace won't draw, and the smoke pours out into the cabin rather than up the chimney. I took pains to do it right.

Building the cabin itself took four days. When I was finished it was only a single room, ten feet square, with a seven-foot ceiling at the front, sloping down to five feet at the rear. It had a dirt floor that I hoped to cover with animal hides over the next few weeks. There was one small door and a single, shuttered window.

It was a long way from being fancy, but I built it tight and caulked every opening with a mixture of clay and grass. It would keep me warm and dry until spring.

The biggest chore after that was keeping enough firewood chopped to stay ahead of the fireplace. They say a man who chops his own wood warms himself twice, and there's more than a little truth to that.

After a few days in the cabin I discovered the chimney didn't draw as well as I thought it would, so I spent a whole day tinkering with it until I got it right.

A week later I started the large cabin. If all went as planned, it would be finished by the middle of March, but counting on something that far away left a lot of room for error.

There was plenty of other work to do as well. One or two

days a week I went hunting, wanting both the fresh meat and the hides, but mostly I worked on the cabin and the claims.

The claim along Whitewood Creek was probably the most important, but for the most part it was just too difficult to work in the winter. I dug enough gravel to make the claim appear used, and left it at that. In my working I pulled maybe thirty dollars' worth of gold dust out of the gravel.

On the second claim I started the first hardrock mine in Deadwood Gulch. Placer mining usually gives way to hardrock mining after a couple of years—it takes that long to pan and sluice the easy gold. Then you get to real mining.

But I wasn't in the mood to wait a couple of years. My experience was in hardrock mining, and I started hacking away at that quartz vein with my pick. I also bought a double-jack from a miner who allowed he didn't need it. Rightly speaking, I needed a single-jack, a couple of drills, and some dynamite. But I made out fairly well with what I had, or could make. The rock was fairly soft and easily worked, so like I said, I made do.

The hole in the rock slowly deepened, and the quartz vein showed gold, though never very much. It was enough, however, to keep me digging. Most of the other miners gave me a funny look when I told them what I was up to, but miners are a pretty independent bunch by nature, so they overlooked what they considered to be my foolishness at digging hardrock when so much easy gold lay about just waiting for the spring thaw.

A good bit of the time it was too damn cold to work, and then I'd socialize a bit. But mostly I worked.

No, mostly I thought and worried about Mary Kay. February came, and the first week of that month was when Mary Kay was expecting to give birth. I wanted to be with her, and couldn't. I wanted to write her a letter, but had no way to post it. So I thought about her, dreamed about her, and worried myself half to death.

Hard work was the only thing that helped take my mind off her even a little bit, so I worked like a dog.

Then came a day when I stepped outside the cabin early one morning and the sun like to have fried me. It must have been forty degrees, and the snow was melting fast. I'd lost track of the exact date, but someone said it was the first of March, or a bit later.

Three weeks later it warmed up to stay. When I took account of how well I did over the winter I was pleasantly surprised. The large cabin was finished except for some minor touches, the hardrock shaft was down twenty feet, and the gold pulled from it weighed in at three hundred dollars.

The spring thaw allowed everyone to start working their claims for real. Whitewood Creek swelled with water, and Deadwood Gulch came alive.

New miners flocked in as I knew they would. They came by ones and by twos, by tens and by twenties. In only a few weeks more than a thousand miners were working the area. Deadwood Gulch was the center of attention, but surrounding gulches were also worked and given their own names such as Whitewood, Gold Run, Blacktail, Whitetail, and Grizzly Gulch.

On the heels of the miners came the less desirable element. Prostitutes, gamblers, saloon keepers, gunhands, claim jumpers, murderers, thugs, and thieves came in numbers to equal the miners. Soon every inch of unworked ground sprouted a tent, and wood frame buildings followed.

Deadwood Gulch was booming. It smelled of gold and easy wealth, and the vultures came to collect their share. Me, I worked my claims, kept my mouth shut, and tried my best to stay away from trouble.

CHAPTER 6

I'D seen cow towns boom before, but it was nothing compared to Deadwood. From a population of less than one hundred over the winter, the area swelled to nearly five thousand by May, and more coming all the time.

And almost overnight Deadwood became a town. Tents sprouted like spring flowers, and by May streets were laid out and wood buildings grew in the midst of the white canvas tents. Some buildings were made of logs, but a surprising number were timber framed and covered with sawn boards.

From the first you could buy whiskey out of a tent, but a couple of fellows named Ike Brown and Craven Lee built a saloon of logs. It was no more than fourteen feet by twenty feet, but they did a booming business.

P. A. Gushurst and William Conners started a general store in a tent, but soon built a wood-frame store on the spot. James W. Wood even started a bank bearing his name. He had an iron safe for storing valuables and also bought gold from the miners at two dollars an ounce less than the twenty you could get in Denver.

Businesses were coming in faster than a man could count them. One old-timer told me that Deadwood Gulch might have plenty of gold from the grass roots down, but it looked like there was even more gold from the grass roots up.

Thinking he might be right, I used my three hundred dollars to buy two lots in town. Then, seeing another opportunity, I used nearly all the gold I'd panned since spring to buy a third lot on Main Street for four hundred dollars.

That left me nearly broke, but a week later I sold both

small lots for five hundred dollars each. Seemed like the old-timer knew what he was talking about.

Mary Kay hadn't left my mind for a minute, but I still hadn't found a way to get word to her. Then a rider came in from Cheyenne, and he brought nearly two hundred letters with him. He gave them to P. A. Gushurst and they were distributed from the store. One of the letters was from Mary Kay.

She'd given birth to a baby boy on the third day of February. His name was Brennan James Darnell. Nothing ever made me feel better than reading that letter. Mary Kay said she missed me, and wondered when I'd be home.

Well, that was a question. I'd a bit over a thousand in my pocket and a good lot on Main Street. I also had the claim along the Whitewood, plus the second outside the area. There was also a third claim I'd marked the day before, but it wasn't a likely prospect. It ran along a trickle of water that emptied into Whitewood Creek and was maybe a quarter mile north of Deadwood. I claimed in because I found a trace of color while panning there, and because with the way land was being grabbed, if I didn't get it someone else would.

Things were actually looking pretty good, but I was still way short of the cash I needed for another go at ranching, and I still didn't know how long it would take to earn it.

With the coming of spring the Sioux took exception to all the miners flooding the area and went on the warpath. Getting to Deadwood was now a fighting proposition, and by the first of June nearly fifty men had been killed coming over the trails. Large groups were fairly safe, and Deadwood was in no danger, but a man going out alone was taking his life in his hands.

There was also trouble within Deadwood. No more than a quarter of the population worked for themselves or anyone else. Sharpers of every stripe flocked to what they hoped would be easy pickings. Usually the good men in a town, even a booming cow town, will outnumber the bad. That wasn't the case in Deadwood. An entire area west of Main Street and along Wall Street was soon nicknamed the "Badlands," and it was there a man went if he wanted a prostitute or a game of cards.

Seldom a night passed without a shooting or a stabbing, though most never made the official reports. I'd thought about having Mary Kay come to stay with me, but Deadwood was a hard, dangerous town, and no place for a woman and a child. I wrote and told her as much, sending out the letter the same way hers had arrived.

I kept working my claims and hustling lots in Deadwood, making a better living than I ever had, but still not pulling in all I needed. Then, on June twenty-second, Custer and most of his command were massacred near the Little Bighorn. It took a week or so for the word to reach us, but when it did there was near panic.

But even in the midst of panic, work continued and Deadwood still grew. By the end of July Deadwood had several hotels, theaters, blacksmith shops, and general stores. One fellow told me he'd personally counted a hundred and ten saloons and was certain he'd missed a few.

The Grand Central Hotel was probably the most decent of the lot, while the Bella Union and the IXL were the most disreputable. The Grand Central had a cook named Lucretia Marchbanks, though most of her customers called her Aunt Lou, or Mahogany. She was a handsome black woman who could put together a meal like nobody I'd ever met.

Jack Langrishe's theater was a good one, reputable and clean. Other theaters brought in minstrels and troupes of women vulgar enough to make a mountain man blush, but Langrishe always had a class act. I saw *Hamlet* performed there, and while I couldn't make out head nor tail of the language, it was still exciting enough to keep me sweating.

The Indian war showed no sign of letting up, and people were nervous, if not scared. Miners who rode out of Deadwood often failed to reach their destination alive, especially if they carried gold. Some of the killing was certainly done by Indians, but more and more it began to appear that an organized group of white men were doing their share of the murdering, and placing the blame on marauding Sioux.

One man's name was mentioned most in connection with the killing, a gambler named Collin Driscoll, and he operated from a saloon in the heart of the Badlands. The saloon was called the Saratoga, and it had all the vice any man could wish for.

Out front you could play keno, poker, or roulette, and a much larger poker game was held in a back room nearly every evening. Out front the pretty girls who waited on the tables were ready and willing to go upstairs if the price was right.

None of that held any interest for me, so I kept my nose to the grindstone and stayed away from the Badlands. I had three claims to work, and most days I panned gold from daylight till dark. But when it rained, or sometimes after dark, I'd work the tunnel up behind the cabin.

Panning for gold is backbreaking work. Gold is heavy and sinks to bedrock, so before you can get the gold, you first have to dig down to bedrock. Luckily, the bedrock was only a few feet down and not overly wet. That helped.

Deadwood Gulch held fortunes in its gravel, and a few collected. By September, one claim, Wheeler Brothers number two below Discovery, had surrendered nearly half a million dollars' worth of gold dust. Then, thinking it was played out, they sold the claim on September eighth for three thousand dollars. The new owners took thirty-two hundred from the ground on the first day they worked it.

Fourteen claims produced from thirty to one hundred thousand dollars by that same date, and a number of men grew rich. But the average miner barely made wages. One of the bankers got together with a mining expert and figured that the average pan held from two to fifty cents in gold dust, and if you divided all the gold found so far by the number of miners, it came to a thousand dollars per man.

But if you subtracted all the gold produced by the three largest claims, it dropped to a hundred dollars per man. If you subtracted all the gold from the fourteen largest claims, it dropped all the way to a dollar a man.

A few were getting rich, a couple of hundred were getting by, but most were in worse shape than when they arrived.

I was somewhere in the middle. By September twenty-fifth, when the first Concord stage rolled into Deadwood, I had seven thousand dollars in the bank, five hundred on me, and a bit more coming each day.

That night I went to the theater with Owen Newberry and saw *The Merchant of Venice*. It was even better than *Hamlet*.

After the play I went back to Owen's cabin with him. Thomas and Henry Walsh came over and we ate a bit, drank a bit, played cards a bit, and talked a lot. They were all doing reasonably well on their claims but in no danger of getting rich.

After a spell, we started talking about our families, and we all agreed that only the thought of striking a fortune kept up in Deadwood. Although I liked to think that getting rich was the farthest thing from my mind, I realized I was only fooling myself.

The truth was, I could sell my claims and have the ten thousand I needed, and maybe a good bit more. Right then I made up my mind. I'd work the claims for one more month, then sell out and head home before hard winter set in again.

When I walked back to my cabin that night and curled up on my cot all alone, I knew my decision was the right one. Next morning I sat down and wrote Mary Kay a letter, telling her I'd be home sometime in December, allowing for another few weeks in Deadwood, and several weeks of travel time.

Then I had breakfast, posted the letter, and went to work on my claims.

Many of the more industrious miners had built sluices, and I thought about it myself. But in the end I decided not to, knowing that not sluicing my claims would actually increase their value when it came time to sell them.

Gold pans are made of soft steel so they can rust easily, and mine was pitted just right. The roughness of the rust catches the tiny particles of gold, but allows dirt and gravel to wash out of the pan.

Working myself half to death that day, I found a crack in the bedrock that contained almost six hundred dollars in gold dust. That crack proved a lucky one, because I found myself a buyer in hitting it.

His name was Zachary Dunbar, and his own claim was a good one, but he wanted more. He drifted over to my claim about twenty minutes before I cleaned out that seam in the bedrock, and he was watching when I washed it out. Right on the spot he offered me five thousand for the claim, and I snapped up his offer.

Next day we went to the bank and took care of business, and by ten that morning I'd almost doubled my money. And I still owned two claims, plus a good lot on Main Street.

I had more than twelve thousand dollars, and by selling out I could probably come close to fifteen thousand. Waiting another month was no longer necessary; in a couple of days I could unload the rest of my property, and then I was going home.

I had enough money to start a ranch and raise a dozen children, and just the thought of seeing Mary Kay again was enough to make me breathe hard.

But just when things looked the brightest, Old Man Trouble came to Deadwood and looked me up first thing.

CHAPTER 7

LIKE I said, the Badlands meant trouble, so I stayed away as much as possible. But from time to time I had to walk through the area when going from one place to another and never thought anything about it. That night I was walking from my cabin down to Whitewood Creek, thinking to tell Owen I'd decided to leave early.

The Badlands was mostly saloons, bawdy theaters, gambling houses, cathouses, and several combinations of the above. Inside the saloons music was playing, and now and again I heard cheering and whistling that was likely for the girls dancing the cancan on stage.

Then I walked past the Saratoga, and in a narrow alley alongside it I heard a man's rough voice. "You'll by God do what I paid you to do. When you took the money it sealed the deal . . . unless you want to give the money back?"

"You know I spent most of the money to pay my hotel bill," a second voice replied. "But I'll find a job and pay you back every cent I owe you."

The second voice froze me in my tracks. It was a woman's voice—no, more like a girl's voice. Young-sounding, and full of fear. I looked down the alley and saw a shaft of light where a door was open, and in the light stood a tall, slim, nattily dressed man. He was holding the wrist of a girl, and she obviously didn't like being held.

"You took the money, and you spent it," the man said. "Now it's time to earn it."

"I agreed to sing here, nothing else. My voice is for sale, but that's all you can buy. Now let me *go!*"

Right then I started walking down the alley toward the

47

light. It was no more than fifty feet or so, and in a matter of seconds I was close enough to be seen, only neither of them was paying attention.

The man jerked on the girl's arm, dragging her almost inside the doorway. By that time I was only a few feet away.

"Turn loose of her arm," I said.

That fellow jumped like he'd stepped on a snake, and looked toward me, surprise showing on his face. I was outside the shaft of light, so he likely couldn't see me plainly. I hadn't raised my voice when I spoke, and I guess he didn't get the message, because he just stared at me, squinting a little. He still had his grip on her wrist.

"Turn loose of her arm," I said again.

He snorted and grinned like he couldn't believe what he was hearing. "Mister," he said. "I don't know who you are, but you should know better than to jump into an argument you know nothing about."

"Looks open and shut to me," I said. "You're holding her wrist, and she doesn't want it held. I'm telling you to let go. What else is there to know?"

"My name, for one thing. I'm Collin Driscoll."

"That's nice," I said. "Now I'm going to tell you one last time. Turn loose of her wrist."

I stepped closer as I spoke, stopping no more than three feet away. Instead of letting go, he squeezed harder and the girl winced in pain. Now, I'm a patient man most times, but he'd used up all I had. When he squeezed her wrist I reached over and took hold of his, then squeezed a bit myself.

Driscoll's mouth and eyes both opened wide, and so did his hand. The girl quickly stepped away from him, and I squeezed even harder. He moaned worse than she had. I let go of his wrist and he clutched it with his other hand.

"You bastard," he said. "I don't know who you are, but I'll have you killed for this. I swear it."

"The name's Darnell," I said. "James Darnell. Now that we've been introduced, I advise you to just let it lay."

He said something vulgar, but I'd heard enough. I shoved him hard in the chest with my right hand and he staggered back inside and sat down on the floor with a thump. The door opened outward and I slammed it closed. The girl said something that shaped up like a thank-you, but I cut her off short. "Not now," I said. "Suppose you walk up to the boardwalk there and wait for me. I won't be long."

"But . . . what . . . ?"

"Just do it. Hurry up."

She went to walking and I stepped over so I would be behind the door when it opened again. Sure enough, not more than fifteen seconds later the door flew open and three men charged out. Only they were looking up the alley and I was behind them. I wasn't in the mood to play games.

I thunked the last one with my Colt and he dropped like a rock. The first two heard him fall and started to turn around, but the sound of my Colt being cocked stopped them cold. "Drop your guns or use them," I said. "I don't much care which."

They dropped their guns. "Now the hideouts," I said.

"I don't know what you're talking about," one of them said. "What hideouts?"

"I figure you each have a hideout gun," I said. "I could be wrong, but the only way to know for sure is to shoot you and search your bodies. And if I don't hear two more pistols hit the ground, that's exactly what I'm going to do."

Two more pistols hit the ground. "Now go back inside and tell Driscoll he's had his try. If there's another, I'll come see him personally."

They walked back inside, leaving the unconscious man where he was. For the second time I shut the door, then hustled up the alley to where the girl was waiting.

"How did you know they would try that?" she asked.

"When you've been around coyotes long enough," I said, "you learn how they think. Now let's get out of here before they try something I'm not expecting."

In a few minutes we had the Badlands behind us. Only once we were in a safer section of town, I had no idea what to do next. "Do you have a place to stay?" I asked.

She shook her head, and I asked how much money she had.

"Just three dollars."

"Do you have friends in town?"

Again she shook her head . . . and I scratched mine. It seemed pulling her out of trouble wasn't as tough as figuring out what to do with her now that I had her.

"Don't worry about me," she said. "I'll find someplace to stay. I want to thank you for helping me. I really didn't know Driscoll expected me to . . . to . . ."

"I believe you. But that's a bad section of town, and Driscoll is the worst of a bad lot."

"I know that now. You said your name was James, didn't you?"

"Yes, ma'am. James Darnell. My friends call me Jim."

"My name is Sarah Elizabeth Donahue. I'm pleased to meet you, Jim. I want to thank you again. Now I better go find a place to stay tonight. It's already pretty late."

"How are you going to find a place to stay without money or friends?"

"I don't know. Maybe one of the hotels will let me sleep in the lobby until daylight?"

She started to turn away, and I swore under my breath. "Wait a minute," I said. "Let's go this way."

"Where to?"

"The Grand Central."

"I can't go back to your hotel. It wouldn't be . . . proper."

"It isn't my hotel. I have a cabin outside of town, and that's where I'll stay. But I'm going to get you a room for the night, and tomorrow we'll think of something to do with you."

"That's very kind of you," she said. "But I couldn't let you pay for a room. You've done enough already."

"No, ma'am," I said. "If I let you walk away without a place to stay or any money, then I haven't done nearly enough. Now come on."

She came on. In the light of the hotel lobby I had my first good look at her. I'm not much good at guessing height and weight on a woman, but she looked to be five-five or a bit more, and maybe one-twenty-five on the hoof. She had green eyes, brown hair, and she was pretty as a picture. But even younger than I'd thought.

"How old are you?" I asked.

"Eighteen."

I just looked at her and she blushed a little. "All right, I'm sixteen. But I've been doing a woman's work since I was twelve."

That I could believe. We got her a room, and I asked her to meet me for breakfast. Then I left and walked on down to Owen's cabin. It was late, but a light still showed in his window, so I tapped lightly on the door. It opened all at once and I found myself looking down the barrel of a twelve gauge shotgun. A thing like that can make your stomach do funny things.

Owen recognized me and lowered the shotgun. "Sorry," he said. "I've had a prowler around here three nights running, and I'm getting tired of it."

"Yeah," I said. "I noticed."

We went inside, Owen poured us both a cup of coffee, and we sat down at the table to talk. I told him about selling the claim and about the trouble with Driscoll.

"Might be a good thing, pulling your freight early," he said. "Collin Driscoll's name keeps popping up every time a miner turns up dead, and you could be next on his list."

"I'll stay clear of him," I said. "And I should be gone in a few days."

"You'll stay out of his way, but will he stay out of yours? If I was you, I'd keep my back to the wall and not answer any hails by night."

We talked long enough to drink the coffee left in the pot,

and most of a second. Just as I was ready to leave, I took five hundred dollars from my pocket and dropped it on the table.

"That should cover the stake you and the others put up," I said. "I'm obliged to all of you."

"That stake wasn't meant to be paid back," Owen said. "It was a gift. You saved us several thousand dollars, and maybe our lives as well."

"Maybe, but I still want you to take that and divide it up as you see fit."

"It isn't necessary, and you know it," Owen said. "But you're too dang stubborn to argue with."

We left it at that, and I walked back to my cabin. Before turning in for the night I checked on Cap and the ponies. Cap came to me eagerly and I patted his neck. It seemed he wanted back on the trail as much as I did. "It won't be long now, Cap," I said. "Just a few more days and we'll ride out where the bears walk and the owls hoot."

With that I walked back to my cabin and went to bed. My dreams were pleasant ones of home and Mary Kay.

CHAPTER 8

WHEN I awoke next morning it was raining. It wasn't yet full light, but a man can only stay in bed so long, and I'd a good night's sleep under my belt. So I sat up in bed, scratched my ribs, and yawned. The sound of the rain was a pretty thing.

I washed and shaved, and was about to fix breakfast when I remembered Sarah. I'd promised to meet her for breakfast, but hadn't set a time. Well, it wasn't likely she was up this early, and even if she was, the hotel wouldn't be serving breakfast for another couple of hours. So I put coffee on and heated the beef and beans from last night. It wasn't much, but it would hold me until later.

After eating, I slipped into my leather boots and laced them up, then threw open the door and stood there watching the rain for a spell, a cup of coffee in hand. I've always liked the rain, so long as I don't have to get out in it. I was hoping this one would stop before I had to get out.

It didn't. The one thing I needed and didn't own at the moment was a slicker. I'd had one, but caught it on a sharp limb and ripped it from neck to hip. Like a fool, I threw it away, thinking to buy another. Only I kept putting off actually buying one. Now it was raining and it looked like I was going to get wet.

After a time I put on my hat and a buckskin jacket that might stop part of the rain, and went on out. Cap and the ponies had a shelter of trees at one end of the corral I'd built them, and they were all huddled together against the rain, their hair slick and wet. I fed them, giving Cap a bit extra, then walked on down to the Grand Central.

The rain was coming down just hard enough to wet a man down after a time, but not hard enough to make him hunt cover. The buckskin jacket helped, but some rain still made it down my neck, and from the waist down I was soaked. Nobody in the Grand Central seemed to notice.

I asked at the desk if Sarah had come down yet, and when I was told no, I went up the stairs and knocked gently on her door, half-expecting her to still be asleep. She opened the door at once, fully dressed and looking mighty pretty.

"I wasn't sure what time you would come," she said. "I've been ready for an hour."

"Sorry to keep you waiting, ma'am," I said. "Most folks don't get up as early as I do."

We walked down to the dining room together and ordered breakfast. There wasn't much you couldn't get in Deadwood by that time, and Sarah ordered some kind of fancy omelet along with something she called crepes. They looked like too thin pancakes to me.

I had steak and eggs, along with fresh biscuits and plenty of butter. The Grand Central had mighty fine food, and nobody could deny Aunt Lou could cook. The only thing I had against eating there was the size of the servings. A man had to order double on everything if he wanted to come away with a full belly. Leastways, I did. I don't recall anyone else ever making the same complaint.

When I was finished someone came and took away the empty plates, and I leaned back with a cup of coffee and lit a cigar after asking Sarah if she minded. Sarah ate with the demure manner of a lady and was still picking at her food long after I finished.

When she did finish, I leaned forward a little. "Ma'am," I said, "I'm going to be leaving Deadwood soon, and, well, I wouldn't feel right going off and leaving you without the wherewithal to get by."

"That's very kind of you," she said. "But you've already

done more than most men would have. You don't owe me anything."

"Maybe, but I still wouldn't feel right. I thought about it some this morning, and I'd like you to take my cabin after I'm gone. I built it to last, not knowing how long I'd be here. It's a fine place."

I took an envelope from my pocket and laid it near her hand. "There's a deed in there to a lot on Main Street that should bring a thousand dollars if you wait for the right buyer. There's also enough cash to get you through for a spell. That's about all I can think to do for you."

Her face was open and her eyes were bright. "All? It's too much! You can't, you shouldn't—"

Then her face hardened. "I'm very grateful," she said. "And I don't mean to hurt your feelings, but I have to tell you the same thing I told Driscoll. If you're expecting anything, well, anything from me, I'm still not for sale."

I felt my face redden. "Ma'am," I said. "You're almighty pretty, but that was the last thing on my mind. Truth is, I have a wife back in Colorado. Her name is Mary Kay, and she's really something, ma'am. I'm not much good at putting my feelings into words, but there just ain't . . . isn't . . . another woman in the world for me. I mean that."

Sarah smiled. "Yes, I can see that. I'm sorry if I offended you. Your Mary Kay is a very lucky woman."

"I don't know about that, ma'am. But I know I'm the luckiest man in the world to have her."

A hand slapped down on my shoulder at that moment, and I looked up to see Owen Newberry. "You just now getting up and about?" I asked. "You'll never get rich that way."

"Huh," he grunted. "You've a lot of room to talk. Here I've put in two hours of hard work in the rain, and I find you having breakfast with a beautiful lady. Bet you'd set here all day if nobody built a fire under you."

"I might at that," I said. "It beats sloshing around in the mud on a day like this."

"I can't argue with that. Aren't you going to introduce me to your friend?"

"I don't know," I said. "I've sort of taken her under my wing, kind of told her I'd keep the undesirable elements in town away from her. What would she think if the first thing I do is introduce you?"

"She'd think you were a man with uncommon good sense," Owen said. "Letting her know you have friends somewhat higher in class than you are."

I laughed and introduced Owen to Sarah. He sat down at the table with us and ordered a breakfast of his own. And I have to admit, Sarah seemed to like him right off. Well, Owen was a fine-looking man, and a decent one to boot. Sarah could do a lot worse. So could Owen, for that matter.

After a time I stood up. "You two can set and talk all day," I said, "but if I don't get with it I'm going to be in Deadwood forever."

Sarah took my hand and thanked me again. Then I walked out of The Grand Central and stood for a minute under the protection of the balcony. It was still raining, though not hard enough to keep folks from bustling along with their business. But it was hard enough to make me think twice about how to spend the rest of the day.

I still had the claim along the small stream up from the gulch, and it had been my thought to spend the day panning it. But working in the rain has never been something I enjoyed. Short of it was, I decided to spend the day working in the mine shaft instead.

It might be dark, damp, and cold in there, and it might cave in on my head at any moment, but at least it was out of the rain.

On the way there I stopped by the general mercantile and bought a case of dynamite, along with a hundred feet of fuse and a box of blasting caps. I also picked up a couple of drills and a single jack. Carrying all of that back to the mine shaft, I lit a lantern and went inside.

The vein of gold was still going, but it had narrowed a bit and seemed to be changing direction. The rock was hard and slow going with only a pick, and I knew it was time to blast. I could have brought in a few buyers and showed them the vein, letting them take their chances on how deep it went, but the truth was, I wanted to know myself.

The hardest part of blasting is drilling the holes to slide the dynamite into. For that I used a small drill and a single-jack. A single-jack is just a small sledgehammer made to swing with one hand, and while not as fast as using a double-jack and a large drill, a good man can still punch a hole in the rock in less time than most would believe.

Taking my time, I drilled three holes in a semicircle around the vein, each hole deep enough to take two sticks of dynamite. Then I sat down to catch my breath and get the dynamite ready for the holes.

Dynamite was something I'd worked with several times, and I knew it wasn't dangerous in and of itself. Not if it was fresh and cool. Dynamite is nothing more than nitroglycerin mixed with an absorbent substance like sawdust or chalk to stabilize it. Like I said, when dynamite is fresh, it isn't dangerous. But when it gets old it starts to sweat, and every drop of sweat is pure nitroglycerin. When it gets like that it can blow if you so much as sneeze around it.

Blasting caps are another story. A blasting cap is fulminate of mercury, and sensitive as a beautiful woman with a wart on her nose. One spark, one sudden blow, and a blasting cap can explode in your hand, taking off several fingers.

So if a man is smart, he fuses the caps before inserting them into the sticks. If one blows you don't want a stick of dynamite going off with it. That could ruin your whole day.

The fuse I had was supposed to burn a foot every thirty seconds, so I cut three pieces of fuse, each piece six feet long. I slipped each piece into the end of a blasting cap and gently crimped the cap together, locking the fuse in place. The caps I slipped into three sticks of dynamite. All that remained was sliding an unfused stick into each hole, then the fused sticks in on top. With the ends of the fuse twisted together, I struck a match, touched it to the fuses, and ran like hell.

It took a full minute to get outside the mine, and two more minutes before the dynamite blew. When it did, I felt the ground rumble a bit, and watched as a cloud of dust and smoke burped out of the mine shaft.

Waiting fifteen minutes for the dust to settle, I went back into the mine, carefully checking the ceiling as I walked. Sometimes blasting can loosen an entire section of the ceiling, and tons of rock can fall without warning.

The roof of the cave was fine, but when I came to the blasting site I was in for a big disappointment. The face had sheered off perfectly, collapsing about a ton of rock onto the floor, but where the gold vein should have been was only smooth rock. It didn't take long to figure out what had happened.

At some time in the past, an earthquake or something had caused the mountain to surge upward, and in the process the vein of gold was cut in half.

It wasn't an uncommon occurrence, but it was a damned exasperating one. Trouble was, that vein of gold might be within a few feet of where I stood, or it might be a hundred yards away, up, down, left, or right, depending on which way the mountain had surged. Finding it again was just barely possible, but so unlikely that it really wasn't worth the effort. Especially since the vein hadn't been all that good to begin with.

Losing the vein of gold didn't mean anything to me in the sense that I was going to stay and mine it anyway, but it did mean I wasn't going to find a buyer. There wasn't a man in Deadwood fool enough to buy a mine showing no trace of gold.

So I cleaned up what little gold was in the rubble and boarded up the mine. Might be somebody with plenty of

time on their hands would come along one day and find the lost vein. But it wasn't going to be me.

Two days later I found a man who was willing to give me a thousand dollars for my last claim. I snapped it up on the spot. I sold the ponies, turned the cabin over to Sarah, said my farewells to Owen and the Walshes. Then I saddled Cap and rode out of Deadwood, pointing south toward Colorado.

Inside my blanket roll I had fifteen thousand dollars in paper money, and another five hundred was tucked inside my vest pocket. It was more than enough to start a good ranch, but as I rode away from Deadwood, that was the last thing on my mind.

Mary Kay, as always, was foremost in my thoughts, and now that I was going back to her the thoughts were stronger and more vivid than ever. I thought of the softness in her eyes when she smiled, the flash of fire in them when she was riled, and the way they were always filled with love. I thought of her hair, brownish red, and the way it blew in the wind. I thought of the softness of her tiny hands, and the warmth of her on a cold night.

Yes, a ranch was a fine thing, but all the land and cattle in the world didn't mean a thing without Mary Kay.

And thoughts of the child I'd never seen were in there with her. I had a son. A son that I'd felt growing beneath my hand, but had never seen.

Maybe it was the thought of Mary Kay and my son that kept me from being quite as careful as usual. Or maybe I was just up against some fellows who were better in the wild than I was. But on the third day out of Deadwood, I had a careless moment, and I paid for it.

CHAPTER 9

SOMETIMES I wasn't sure who chose to ride the wild trails, Cap or myself. I loved the high lonesome. I enjoyed being out where perhaps no white man, and maybe no Indian, had ever stepped. But Cap seemed to pick those trails as instinctively as I did. Had I tried to turn him away, I'd the hunch he would have been sorely disappointed.

With no ponies and no gear to worry about, I pushed hard and fast, picking the wildest, loneliest stretches of country I could find, hoping to avoid contact with white man and red alike.

But along about dark of the first day out, the thought came to me that I was being followed. There was nothing solid to back up the feeling. Once I saw what might have been a flash of sunlight off a belt buckle a mile or so back . . . or might as easily have been a reflection from a piece of quartz in the rock.

Another time I saw a hint of movement. It might have been an animal—a deer or an elk, or it might have been a horse. It was simply too far away to tell. Either way, it should have been enough to warn me, to make me circle back and watch my trail for a time. But I was still thinking about Mary Kay and getting home. I kept riding.

The second day out I saw nothing and let myself be convinced the whole notion was foolish. On the third day I stopped along about noon and built a small fire. I made coffee and a bit of lunch, ate, repacked everything but the coffeepot, and took a short walk around to stretch my muscles.

It was wild, mountainous, ruggedly beautiful country, and

I liked it. Off about two hundred yards from my fire was a slope that couldn't really be called a cliff, but it was a fine place to look over the land. Taking a cup of coffee, I walked to the edge of the slope, lit a cigar, and just stood there looking around.

The cool air felt good, and so did the warm sun that fought it. A bird of some kind fluttered in a small tree off to my left. Fifty yards down the gentle slope, a ground squirrel darted into the open and scampered about, looking for food.

A hawk screamed and dived on the squirrel. The squirrel dashed for safety, but came in too slow. The diving hawk struck, razor sharp talons and strong beak making short work of the prey.

Standing there just watching the country was a fine thing, and I could have done it for hours without tiring. But the call of home and Mary Kay was too strong to ignore. Tossing the last half inch of coffee in my cup, I turned to walk back to camp. The turn saved my life.

I was halfway into the turn when the bullet struck me in the leg. My leg went out from under me and I fell hard. As I turned I'd stepped up onto a small rim of rock that led away from the slope. In doing that I'd raised my body at least a foot and a half. So I'd taken the bullet in the leg rather than in the gut.

In falling, I slid back right to the edge of the slope and stopped myself from going over only by grabbing at a handhold. But I saw the smoke from the rifle and felt fairly certain that I couldn't be seen from there while lying flat. Then I saw the second man.

He popped up from nowhere, only fifty yards to my left, nearly at the edge of the slope himself. He had a rifle in hand, and it was aimed right at me.

I just turned loose of my handhold and pushed off, letting myself go over the edge of the slope. The man fired and the bullet struck rock where my head had rested only a moment earlier. Then I was rolling and bouncing down the slope.

It wasn't anything like a fall, but it was steep enough to let me pick up a bit of speed. Too much speed. I rolled and tumbled and somersaulted, slamming into a rock outcropping and cracking my head hard enough to stun me.

For a few seconds I lay there, trying to fight off a wave of nausea. My head was pounding and my leg hurt like hell, but I knew I had to move. Getting my good leg under me, I pushed off hard, trying to get behind the rock outcropping. A bullet tugged at my shirt near the collar and struck the rock right next to my head. A fragment of the rock hit me above the left eye. I felt blood running down my face.

I fell, coming to rest behind the rock, out of sight from above. A wave of darkness rushed over me, receded, came again. Then I heard someone yell, "I tell you, Denny, that last shot got him. Looked like it hit him right in the head."

"Maybe," a second voice replied. "But I want to see for myself. Besides, he might have all the money on him. I ain't about to ride off and leave it down there with a dead man."

For a time there was silence. Then rocks rattled. My Colt was cocked and in my hand, though I couldn't remember drawing it. I didn't think I could see well enough to hit anything, but it looked like I was going to have to try.

Then the first voice swore loudly. "They're coming this way," the second voice said. He sounded very close.

"Let's get his horse and ride the hell out of here," one of the men said. "I didn't bargain for a fight with them."

Blackness washed over me again, and time seemed to stop. I heard horseshoes striking rock, retreating into the distance, and I tried to sit up enough to look around. I almost made it, but fell back and hit hard. Five minutes or more passed, and the sounds of more horses came to me. Something was wrong, but I didn't know what it was. Then I realized the horses weren't making as much noise as they should have been.

Why was that? They seemed close enough. Why weren't they loud enough? Then it came to me. The horses were unshod. Indian ponies. It had to be. White men wouldn't be out here riding unshod ponies.

There was no more sound for several minutes. Then a soft scraping sound came to my ears, and of a sudden a Sioux warrior was standing over me, rifle pointed right at my nose. Then a wave of blackness larger and deeper than the others swept over me. For a long time I knew nothing at all.

CHAPTER 10

MY eyes opened, but I couldn't move, and I had no idea where I was. My head throbbed with pain, and my leg was almost as bad. Or maybe worse. It didn't seem to matter. At last my hand moved, coming up to my face. My fingers probed and felt a growth of beard that shouldn't have been there. Then I passed out again, but not before I had an odd thought. *A teepee* my mind said. *Damned if this place doesn't look like an Indian teepee.*

Consciousness came and went, then I opened my eyes and an Indian woman had my head propped up and was pouring something into my mouth. I swallowed. Whatever it was tasted good. I drank the wooden bowl empty and she eased my head down. She left the teepee, and a minute later Eyes-Like-Water came in.

She sat down beside me, but I had to try two or three times before I could speak. When I did get the words out, harsh and brittle, they sounded like words spoken by a stranger. But I managed to ask how bad off I was, how long I'd been in the camp.

"You have been here almost a week," Eyes-Like-Water said. "One of the men in the war party was at the cave. If he had not recognized you they would have killed you. I . . . your leg is pretty bad. It's broken, but it's also sick. Infected, I think you call it."

I nodded a little. "I have a fever. Need to see a doctor. Can you get me to Deadwood?"

"No. We can't go near there. We have only a few men."

"Can you get me close to Deadwood? Along a trail where I'll be found?"

For a minute she said nothing. Then, "I will ask. Perhaps that is possible."

She stood up. "Is Black Eagle here?" I asked. "I'd like to see him."

Her eyes avoided mine. "Black Eagle is dead. The soldiers killed him in the fight with your Custer."

"I'm sorry to hear that."

Eyes-Like-Water simply nodded. She turned around and went outside. For an hour I was left alone. It seemed longer. When she finally returned she brought water with her. It tasted wonderful.

"We will take you to a trail where you can be found," Eyes-Like-Water said. "It is all we can do."

"When?"

"Morning. It is too late to start today."

Morning was a long time coming. Eyes-Like-Water gave me broth later in the evening, and even a bit of meat, though my stomach didn't quite go along with that. My fever seemed to be getting worse, and several times during the night I slipped into a condition where nothing seemed real.

But morning came at last and two muscular Sioux loaded me onto a travois. I won't say it was an easy ride, but the shock of pain that went through me every time the travois bumped over a rock was the only thing that kept me conscious.

We traveled most of the day, stopping three hours or so before dark. Several times throughout the day Eyes-Like-Water helped me drink water, but by the time we stopped my mouth felt dry and I was burning up.

"This is not the main trail," Eyes-Like-Water said, "but it is used almost every day. Some of us will stay with you until you are found. I'm sorry we can do no more, but your leg is too bad."

Her words seemed to come from an enormous distance. I lost all track of time, and didn't know if we stayed near the trail for an hour or for a day. But suddenly Eyes-Like-Water was beside me. "Several white men are coming," she said. "They have a wagon and should be able to take you without trouble. We will watch from cover until we know."

Then she was gone. A wagon rolled up twenty minutes later . . . or twenty hours later. I heard men speaking among themselves, but the words seemed fuzzy. I closed my eyes for a moment to rest.

The next time I opened my eyes everything was clear. It took only a moment to realize I was in my own cabin, but I hadn't the faintest idea how I might have gotten there. Instinctively, I tried to sit up. My muscles tightened, but they simply lacked the strength to raise my body. I rested, and after a time tried again. This time I made it up to one elbow, but that was it.

Dropping back to the pillow, I grunted loudly. A couple of minutes later the door opened and Sarah Donahue came in. She was wearing an apron and wiping flour from her hands. When she saw that my eyes were open she gasped. "I can't look that bad," I said. "Or can I?"

She didn't bother to answer, but turned around and ran from the room. Seconds later I heard the front door open and close. Might be I looked that bad after all.

Something like half an hour passed and I heard the front door again. This time when Sarah came in she wasn't alone. She had Owen Newberry and a doctor with her. Owen sat down and watched with a worried look on his face while the doctor checked my leg, then poked and probed every conceivable place he could find.

"Am I going to live?" I asked.

"It looks like it," he said. "I don't see how, and two weeks ago I wouldn't have given a poke of brass filings for your chances, but yes, it looks like you'll live. So either I'm a better doctor than I thought, or you're just too damn muleheaded to die."

"Likely a little of both," I said. "How bad is the leg?"

"The leg wasn't the problem," he said. "It had a bullet in it, and the bone was broken, but it was a nice, clean break and should heal nicely.

"No, the problem was infection. The bullet probably carried it into the wound, and from there it spread throughout your body. You should have died."

"How soon can I get out of this bed?"

He snorted. "Don't plan on getting up anytime soon. The wound in your leg should be healed in another week or two, but the bone is going to take longer.

"In a month you can get around with crutches, or even a cane, but I don't want you to try getting out of bed, not even just into a chair, for three weeks."

"Three weeks! That's a lifetime, Doc, and I have things to do!"

"And for the first time it looks like you'll have a chance to do them," he said. "But if you try to get up from that bed too soon you might lose all the ground you've gained. So stay put."

"He'll stay put," Sarah said. "I'll see to that."

The doctor left soon after that, and Sarah asked if I was hungry. I told her yes and she went out to fix something. Owen pushed his hat back and shook his head. "Beats me how one man can get into so much trouble," he said. "What happened out there anyway?"

I told him all I could remember. "Thing is," I said, "I should have known better. I knew I was being followed. I knew it. But I was too anxious to get home."

"Maybe. We all make mistakes, though."

"They took my money," I said. "Fifteen thousand dollars. Money that was intended to build a ranch and raise a family. I have a wife back there, Owen, and a child I've never seen. That money was for them."

"I know. But what can you do about it?"

"Nothing, maybe. But I intend to try. I got part of a name on one of them, and they took Cap. That was a mistake. A horse like Cap is easy to spot anywhere. If I find him, I'll find the men who shot me."

"That's an idea in itself," Owen said. "There's mining camps all up and down these hills now. If we put out a description of Cap, someone might spot him. People will be glad to help. They've had enough of these ambushes."

"I've had enough," I said. "Next time around it's going to be my turn to name the tune and let somebody else dance."

"You find the men who did it," Owen said, "be sure to let me know. I'd like a piece of them myself. But go careful until you're strong enough to hold a gun."

"What do you mean?"

"Just that Deadwood isn't all that large a city yet. Word will get around that you're going to live, and when it does, somebody might try to finish the job."

"You think the men who ambushed me are still around?"

"Why wouldn't they be? Hell, man. They left you in the middle of nowhere, thinking you were dead. Might be they even have ties here in Deadwood that would make leaving tough. Any chance you'd recognize either of them if you saw them again?"

I shook my head. "No. I only saw the one, and he was fifty yards away. I doubt I'd even know their voices, but there's always a chance."

For a time Owen was silent. Then he took a lungful of air and let it out. "Hell, Jim," he said. "I done something that seemed right at the time, but now I'm afraid I really messed things up."

"It can't be that bad."

"Better wait until you hear what it is," he said. "When they brought you in, the doc said you didn't have a chance. He expected you to die anytime, and said there just wasn't any way you could last out the week."

"So?"

"So I wrote a letter to your wife. I didn't tell her you were dying, exactly. But I did say you'd been shot and were in a bad way."

"Damn," I said. "When Mary Kay gets that letter she'll come to Deadwood as fast as she can."

"Maybe not. Might be she'll wait to see if another letter comes."

"I doubt it. You don't know her. She's the best woman I've ever known, but when she gets a thing in her head, she doesn't waste time in the doing."

"I'm sure sorry," Owen said. "I didn't mean to worry her, but you were in such bad shape that, well, I thought she would want to know."

"It's all right," I said. "You had no way of knowing I was going to make it. I'd have done the same thing in your shoes. But if you'll help, I'd like to get another letter off to her as soon as possible. Might be it'll reach her before she takes off."

"The way mail travels, it might," Owen said, "but I wouldn't bank on it."

I wouldn't have either, but trying was all we could do. Owen wrote the letter, with me telling him pretty much what to say. Once the letter was finished, we talked a spell longer, then Owen left to post the letter and take care of other business.

Sarah brought some food in to me then, and much as it shames me to admit it, she had to spoon-feed me a part of it. I was still that weak.

By the time I had a bit of food in my stomach, even with Sarah doing most of the work, I was done in. Sleep came instantly, and it was morning before I awoke. Sheriff Seth Bullock came by along about noon, and I repeated my story to him. He allowed that Cap was the only real lead, and even at that, it would take luck to ever catch the men who'd shot me.

There wasn't much I liked about it, but I had to agree with him.

"Trouble is," he said, "they'll know you're alive before long, and that your horse could mean trouble for them. Like as not they'll either drive him clean out of the territory to sell, or they'll shoot him."

"If it has to be one or the other," I said, "I hope they sell him."

Sheriff Bullock promised to do his best, shook my hand, and left. After that Raymond, Thomas, and Henry Walsh came by to see how I was doing. Sarah ran them off after a spell, saying I was still weak and needed my rest. She was right.

That second day I got the first good look at myself. It wasn't a pretty sight. My face was thinner, almost gaunt, and there were dark circles under both eyes. I'd lost weight, too. Fifteen pounds or more, and it made me look mighty poor.

I knew good food and hard work would put the meat back on my bones, but I also knew I had to wait for my leg to begin mending before I could do anything. That was the hardest part of all. It had been mid-September when I was shot, and three weeks had already passed. It didn't take much figuring to realize it would be November before I was even hobbling around with a cane, if the doctor was right, and probably December before I was anything like my old self.

But there was nothing for it. All I could do was wait, so I waited.

CHAPTER 11

I PUSHED the doctor's orders as much as possible, but it was still two weeks before I moved to a chair, and that with help. But a week later I was hobbling about on crutches, and within ten more days I was able to do a pretty good job with a cane.

My first trip out of the cabin came on December sixth. The telegraph made its way to Deadwood on the first of December, but it was the sixth before I had enough sense to use it. Bundling up against the cold, and using the cane with a lot less skill than I should have, I hobbled down to the telegraph office and sent a message back to Colorado.

There was no way to send a message directly to Mary Kay or Pa, of course, but the town of Pueblo was only a few miles from the ranch, and the sheriff there was a friend of mine. I sent the wire to him, asking if he would ride out and check on Mary Kay. If she was still there he was to tell her I was doing fine and that she shouldn't try to come to Deadwood.

By the time I made it back to the cabin my left leg was tired and sore, but the old throbbing pain was gone. The doctor came to take a look at my leg every ten days or so, and he said it was healed about as well as it ever would be. Now I had to use it and build the strength back up.

Too, I'd gained back a good bit of the weight lost in the weeks of being sick, but I still looked a little peaked. No matter—my appetite was back, and food was something I couldn't seem to get enough of.

It was time I started looking for Cap and for the men who shot me. Better than two months had passed, and the trail was already long cold. Truth was, I didn't really know where to start. But it wasn't in me to let it go.

A couple of days later a telegram came from the sheriff of Pueblo. He'd ridden out to Pa's ranch and checked on Mary Kay, only to find that she had already left for Deadwood. In fact, she'd been gone some time and should be arriving almost any day.

Sure enough, five days later she came in on the stage, Brennan James with her. Only trouble was, I didn't know she'd be on the stage, so I was still up at the cabin. So was Sarah.

Mary Kay asked about and got directions to the cabin, and she came up on foot. Not being certain she had the right place, she knocked before coming in. Sarah answered the door. Me, I was in the kitchen and didn't hear any of this going on, but they both told me about it later.

Mary Kay didn't say who she was, just asked if Sarah knew where I lived. Sarah, of course, said I lived here. "Oh, I see," Mary Kay said. "And might I ask who you are?"

"My name is Sarah Donahue," Sarah said. "I'm living here with him. Why do you ask?"

Sarah told me that Mary Kay's face went through a whole range of emotions and settled on spitfire mad. "Because," Mary Kay said, "I'm his wife."

With that Mary Kay came into the cabin, going right past Sarah. She came into the kitchen, and I was so happy and surprised to see her that I didn't notice her green eyes were on fire. I was out of my chair and halfway to taking her in my arms before I realized she was madder than a wet hornet. Mary Kay hit me with a look that froze me in my tracks, then pointed at Sarah. "Who," Mary Kay said, "is she?"

I started to introduce Sarah, but just as my mouth opened it dawned on me how the situation must have looked to Mary Kay. I felt my face turn red and my mouth clamped shut. I looked over at Sarah, and her face was every bit as red as mine felt.

For a couple of minutes we both tried to stammer out an explanation, but it didn't sound right, even to me.

"Let me see if I have this straight," Mary Kay said. She pointed at me. "You saved her from a man who tried to make her do things she didn't want to do. Then you felt sorry for her and gave her this cabin, plus a building lot in town. Then you left Deadwood, got yourself shot up, and she took you in to nurse you back to health? Now, you've both been living here together, but nothing has been going on in all this time? Is that what you're trying to tell me?"

Sarah and me looked at each other, then at Mary Kay. We both nodded vigorously. "Yup," I said.

For just a few seconds Mary Kay stood there looking at me, then her face softened. "Well," she said, "if anything was going on, you'd have a better explanation than that one. Anything that lame has to be the truth.

"Only you, James, could get yourself into a situation like this one. Now come here and meet your son."

What I did was come over and hug both of them near to death. I'd tried to stop Mary Kay from coming, but I was almighty glad she was here. When I let Mary Kay up for air, she handed me my son. "Here," she said. "You get to know him while I get to know Sarah."

I took Brennan in my arms and sat down in a chair to ease my leg. He was ten months old, already walking, and cute as a newborn lamb. Mary Kay's hair is brown except when the sun hits it right, then it has a hint of red in it. My own hair is dark brown, and even the sun doesn't lighten it up much. Brennan's hair was blond. He also had dimples.

There's a few special times in a man's life that stand out head and shoulders above the rest. The first time he looks in the eyes of a woman and knows he's in love is one of them. When he marries that woman and makes love to her is another.

But I can't recall anything ever feeling quite like holding my own son for the first time. A big part of the feeling was love, but I have to admit, a big part of it was also fear. I always knew there was a possibility of getting killed, whether by accident or design, but I took it as a matter of course.

Mary Kay was the strongest woman I'd ever known, and she would get by no matter what. If something happened to me she would cry and mourn my loss, but then she'd pick herself up and go on with life.

But holding my son made me afraid. What would happen to him if I should die or be killed? Mary Kay was strong, smart, capable, but how would she handle raising a child all alone?

I really didn't doubt that she could do it, but I knew how terribly difficult it would be. It made a man think.

After a time Brennan began wiggling in my arms and I sat him carefully on the floor. He looked around for a minute, then pulled himself to a standing position and walked over to Mary Kay. He almost fell twice, but caught himself and made the trip standing. Mary Kay was sitting at the other end of the table, talking to Sarah, and when Brennan ran full tilt into her legs she picked him up without looking. He patted her breast and made a sound that she interpreted as, "Nurse, nurse."

Mary Kay undid her blouse and discreetly gave him a breast. He latched onto the nipple like a hungry man grabbing onto a steak. Me, I'd seen calves nurse, and plenty of colts, but a baby was something else again. Mary Kay saw me watching.

"I'll probably wean him in a couple of months," she said. "But not until he's ready. It's too special."

"That it is," I said. "Is that all he eats?"

"Heavens, no! Unfortunately, he seems to have inherited your appetite. So far I haven't found much of anything that he won't eat."

"That's my boy," I said.

After the initial tension, Mary Kay and Sarah hit it off fine. In half an hour they were friends, and soon after that, both started telling stories about me. Not a single story was particularly flattering, but they both sat there telling them and laughing like I was stone-deaf.

"If you two are going to talk about me," I said, "you could at least think of something nice to say."

They both looked at me, then at each other. Then they went back to the stories. They didn't improve enough to notice.

After a time Sarah looked at both of us. "I don't really know how to say this, but I'll try." She looked at me. "When you gave me this cabin and the lot in town you were leaving. That made it . . . all right, somehow. But since you're going to be staying here for a while, especially with your wife and son, I think you should take the things back."

I looked at Mary Kay. She shook her head a little. "No," I said. "This place is yours, and so is the lot in town. This is a big cabin, and if it's all right, we'll stay here for a while at least. But I think you should stay with us. There's plenty of room, and then some."

"That's exactly what I think," Mary Kay said. "We won't get in each other's way. It should work out fine. Besides, could you honestly afford to stay in a hotel?"

"For a while. James gave me some money, and I still have most of that left."

"Why haven't you sold the lot?" I asked. "You must have had offers?"

"A few, but I thought I'd go partners with someone and maybe build on the site myself. Seems to me that's the way to make real money?"

"It is," I said. "I never had the temperament for such work myself. Trying to run a store or the like would drive me crazy. But there's no denying it's where the money is. I wonder how much it would take to build a nice store of some kind and stock it proper?"

"I've asked around some," Sarah said. "I can have a decent building put up for a thousand dollars. But, assuming it's a mercantile, it might cost two or three times that to stock it with goods."

"That's a lot of money," I said. "Have you had any luck in finding a partner?"

"Plenty, if I want to settle for a ten-percent share. It seems no one thinks the land is worth half interest in whatever business goes on top of it. It might be different if I could go ahead and have something built, but I can't afford it."

"What if I could raise the money," I said. "Or enough of it to get started. Would you consider a partnershp?"

"With you? Of course."

"Actually," I said, "it was Mary Kay I had in mind. I meant it when I said that kind of work would drive me crazy, but Mary Kay has always wanted to start some kind of business."

I looked at Mary Kay. "How about it?" I said. "Does it interest you?"

"Yes, it does. But aren't we moving kind of fast? I just got here. Sarah doesn't really know me yet, and you're talking about a lot of money. Correct me if I'm wrong, but weren't you shot and robbed just a while back?"

I smiled. "Good point. But I have to get back on my feet sooner or later. Finding another good claim around here will be harder than pulling teeth. All the good locations were claimed months ago.

"It might be possible to find something that at least pays wages, or I might get lucky and find something rich out in the back of nowhere. It isn't something I can count on, though."

"So you want to start a store? It doesn't sound like you," Mary Kay said. "What brought all this on?"

Brennan was through nursing and sat up.

"I'm still going to look for the men who robbed me," I said. "They took money I need, and they took Cap."

I took Brennan from Mary Kay and held him close to my face. He laughed and grabbed at my nose.

"Maybe it's silly," I said, "but just seeing this little fellow makes me feel . . . different. I still want a ranch, but somehow it doesn't seem as important now. What counts is seeing that he's raised proper."

"I don't think that's silly at all," Mary Kay said. "That's what being a father means."

The three of us talked it over for a time, and we agreed that a partnership was a good idea. I would, somehow, supply the money for building and stocking. Mary Kay and Sarah would run the store, and we would all share fifty-fifty.

It wasn't something I'd thought out, and I wondered if I was getting in over my head. But it seemed we would be in or around Deadwood for a while, at least through the winter, and there was no point in wasting the time.

Sarah stood up. "It might be better if I did stay here," she said. "It would certainly save on money. But for a night or two I think I will stay at the Grand Central. The two of you need some time alone, and that's the least I can do."

I wasn't about to argue that point. I hadn't seen Mary Kay in over a year, a long, long time. I promised myself it would never happen again.

On the other hand, Sarah stretched the two days into a week, and that week with Mary Kay made the last year almost worthwhile. It made me appreciate her all the more and, if possible, made me love her even more than before.

The week ended all too soon and the outside world caught up with us. I didn't like it. I would have been content to stay inside the cabin with Mary Kay until spring.

But the one thing I couldn't do inside the cabin was make money, and we needed money. I wanted the store up and operating by spring, and I still hoped to find the men who stole my money. Most of it was likely spent, but there was still Cap. I didn't like the idea of someone else riding him. I didn't like it at all.

So at the end of the week I reluctantly welcomed Sarah back into the cabin, and I even more reluctantly left it myself.

On that last morning Mary Kay and me stayed in bed uncommon late, just holding each other and talking.

"You've changed," she said. "For the better, I think."

"How's that?" I asked.

She pressed closer against me. "I don't know. You just seem calmer . . . more settled. A year ago you would have been hell-bent to get out and find the men who shot you and stole Cap."

"I'm still going after them."

"I know. But not for the same reasons. A year ago it would have been revenge, and you would have gone white-hot with anger. Now you're going because you think it's the right thing to do . . . and because you still hope to get part of your money back."

"And for Cap," I said. "I'm going after Cap."

She laughed. "Yes, you're going after Cap. I never knew a man could care so much about a horse. If it were possible, I'd think the two of you were related."

"In a way, maybe we are," I said. "Cap has carried me out of more trouble than I could get into. We've been through some rough country and some rough times together. I just wouldn't feel right leaving him out there, not knowing who has him or how he's being treated."

"You do what you have to do," Mary Kay said. "I know the kind of man you are. I know you could never rest if you let someone steal from you and get away with it. It's one of the things I love about you.

"But remember, you have a son now. I want you to see him grow up, and I want him to know you. If you get yourself killed both of you will lose a lot."

"You can bet I'll be careful."

We kissed. It was a long time later before we finally got out of bed, and then only because Brennan began crying. He was well nursed, but we'd been keeping him in a smaller bed at the far side of the room, and he plain got restless. So we got out of bed, dressed, and I took Brennan into the living room to play while Mary Kay made breakfast.

Sarah came along about the time we finished eating, and Owen Newberry knocked on the door twenty minutes after that. He brought with him news that thrust me out into the real world again.

CHAPTER 12

I KNEW something was up when Owen kept insisting we go down to the saloon and have a drink. That wasn't like Owen. Not that he didn't take a drink every now and then, but like me, he preferred to sit and talk and have a drink in one of our cabins.

So I went with him down to Nuttall and Mann's. We both ordered a glass of beer at the bar and walked to an empty table away from the few people there. We drank half our beers without saying a word. "All right," I said finally. "You have something on your mind, Owen. What is it?"

Owen straightened up in his chair and pushed his hat back with his finger. Then he drained his glass and signaled the bartender to bring two more. After a minute the bartender came over, sat two glasses of beer on the table and took Owen's empty glass away. Only then did Owen speak.

"You're right," he said. "Something is on my mind. Truth is, it's been on my mind for a couple of days now. I been debatin' whether or not to tell you, and finally decided there wasn't much choice. You got the right to know, even if it does make you run out and get shot up again."

"Damn it, Owen, if you've something to say, spit it out."

Owen nodded. "Soon as it looked like you were going to live," he said, "I put out word about Cap. This is a big country, but Cap is a hard horse to miss, so I thought there was at least a chance of finding him. Maybe one chance in a hundred, but still a chance.

"Couple of days ago, an old geezer drifted in and looked me up. He'd been scouting for General Crook during the summer, and was laying up in Custer City for the winter.

Only he had occasion to ride out to one of the ranches northeast of here to deliver some supplies.

"On the way back the weather got the better of him, and when he saw what looked to be a dugout off in the distance he naturally headed his team that way, hoping to find a warm place to sleep for the night.

"Turned out the place wasn't really a ranch as he'd thought, just a spot where a couple of men had dug a house into a bank, threw together a brush corral in the shelter of a draw, and were waiting out the winter."

"What does that have to do with Cap?"

"I'm getting to that. Seems the corral these gents built had half a dozen head of horses. Most of them were nothing to look at, but one caught his eye. It was a big horse, just the right color, and it had a bullet scar across the haunch just where Cap did."

My heart was beating faster. "What about a brand?"

Owen shook his head. "The horse was turned the wrong way. Never could get a look."

I drank down the rest of the beer in my glass, then let half the second beer slide down my throat. "It sounds like Cap," I said.

"Yes, it does," Owen said. "It also sounds like quite a few other horses."

"Not many horses around as big as Cap, or such an off shade of roan."

"There's a few," Owen said. "Not many, but a few."

"With a bullet scar in just the right place?"

"I got to admit," Owen said, "that's what set me to thinking. But it's still likely a wild goose chase."

"Maybe. But I'm going out there and have a look. Did you get directions?"

Owen took a piece of folded paper from his pocket and handed it to me. I opened it and found a crude map. Crude, but well enough drawn to get the job done. "Thanks, Owen," I said. "I appreciate it."

"Wait until we find out if it's Cap," he said. "It if pans out, and if you don't get yourself killed, you can thank me then."

I finished my second beer and walked back to the cabin. My left leg still hurt if I walked on it too much, and the cane was still in my hand. But halfway back to the cabin I tossed the cane away. It was time to quit babying myself and make up for lost time.

Mary Kay was waiting on me. When I sat down she went to the kitchen and came back a minute later with a cup of coffee. She handed it to me and sat down next to me. Brennan was sitting on the floor not far away, tossing around a set of wooden blocks that Owen had made for him.

Taking a swallow of the hot coffee, I rubbed my leg, then put my arm around Mary Kay. "I love you," I said.

She snuggled closer to me. "It's going to start again, isn't it?" she asked. "Owen had something to tell you that he didn't want me to hear, and now the trouble is going to start again."

"I don't know," I said. "Maybe."

It didn't take but a minute to repeat what Owen had told me. Mary Kay didn't try to argue with me, but she did stand up and walk to Brennan. She sat down beside him and helped him stack the blocks. Only after a full three minutes did she look back at me.

"I won't try to stop you from going," she said. "I'm afraid that if I asked you not to go, you would listen to me. You'd stay here and try to be a good husband and father, but inside it would eat you alive.

"No, I won't ask you to stay. But I will ask you not to get yourself killed. I know how good you are with a pistol, and I know how strong and brave you are. But, please, for me and for Brennan, try being a little bit afraid?"

Easing out of the chair, I sat down on the floor next to her, moving around until I found a position where my leg didn't ache. "Every time I think about the two of you," I said, "it scares me half to death. Just the thought of never seeing

THE PAYBACK ■ 83

you again, of not being there for Brennan, scares me all the way down to my boots.

"I have to go, Mary Kay. If I don't it won't get done. The only law around here is local. They can't do much about anything that happens outside of town. Out there in the wild, the army is the law, but they have their hands full. They don't have the time or the desire to check on something like this.

"Truth is, I'd just as soon stay right here. But in this country a man has to stand up for himself. If he doesn't the word gets around. A man who backs off from trouble is labeled a coward, and folks won't have much to do with him.

"They say the cowards never started for the Black Hills, the weak died along the way, and the fools went on to Wyoming. It mightn't be right, but that's the way folks think. And when you get right down to it, I guess that's the way I think."

"How soon will you leave?"

"Day after tomorrow, if everything works out. I need to find myself another horse, but I don't want to spend any more than necessary to get a decent one. We need to be pretty tight with a dollar until I find a way to start earning my keep again."

"We'll get by."

"Yes," I said, "we'll get by. But I want more than that. More for you, more for Brennan."

I got up. My leg was asleep and needles ran up and down the length of it. I walked it off, grouching every step.

"I'll never understand men," Mary Kay said. "I've seen you shot and at death's door, and never a complaint. But your leg goes to sleep and you act like you're dying."

I smiled, but my thoughts were more serious. "Mary Kay," I said, "do you like it around here? In Deadwood, I mean?"

She thought a minute. "Yes, I do. I like the town and I like the people. And I've never seen such beautiful country. Why do you ask?"

"Do you like it enough to live here?"

"You mean permanently? I thought you wanted a ranch?"

"I do. But this is as good a place as any to build a ranch. In fact, it's a sight better than most. You should see some of the grassland northeast of here. It's beautiful country, all right.

"The winters are cold. Colder than blue . . . almighty cold. But if a man was smart and cut plenty of hay for the winter, that shouldn't be a problem. I like it here, Mary Kay. I really do.

"It's funny. When I first rode into Deadwood Gulch all I could think of was getting my fortune and getting out. But then I watched the town spring up around me, and now you're here. Yes, ma'am, I like it here."

"Wherever you are," she said, "is where I want to be. I don't care if it's Deadwood or Mexico. I do like it here, though. I've never seen a town quite like this one."

Sarah came in the door, her cheeks red from the cold. Her eyes were bright with excitement. She almost ran to us.

"I know you're worried about money," she said, "but is there a chance you can spare two hundred dollars?"

"What for?"

"Do you know Delmer Higgins?"

"Haven't really met him, but yeah, I know who he is. I guess he's put up as many buildings in Deadwood as anybody. He does good work, too."

"That's right," Sarah said. "But things are a little slow for him now because of the weather. So I got together with him and we worked out a deal. He agreed to put up a building for us, just the kind we want, for a thousand dollars.

"He also agreed to take half the money now, the other half when the work is finished. That will be in three months."

"What happens if we can't come up with the last five hundred?"

"Then he gives us five hundred instead, and he owns the building and the lot it's on."

I thought about it. "I think he's trying to take advantage of you," I said.

"So do I. Five hundred dollars is a lot of money, and he doesn't think I can raise it in time. Mr. Higgins believes he's going to own a very valuable lot in three months' time."

"Then why go along with him?"

"Because I have confidence in you . . . and in myself. I think we can raise the money. But I only have three hundred plus change right now. I need the last two hundred to set things rolling."

I looked at Mary Kay. "I still have to buy a horse," I said. "If we do this we won't have much more than a hundred dollars left, and none coming in."

"But you want to do it?"

"Yes, I do," I said. "Sarah's right. Delmer Higgins thinks he's found a sucker. I think we can beat him at his own game. If the three of us together can't raise five hundred dollars in ninety days, we don't deserve to keep the building or the lot."

I looked at Sarah. "Did you tell him you had a partner?"

"He didn't ask," she said, "so I didn't see any reason to volunteer the information."

"Let's do it," Mary Kay said. "The one thing I've already noticed about this town is how few women there are. I'll bet I can make a good bit of money just sewing and taking in laundry. I've seen more men wearing patches on their clothes than I can remember."

Going to a nook in the kitchen where I kept most of our money hidden, I counted out two hundred dollars and gave it to Sarah. "You know," I said, "the deal was for me to pay for the building."

"Who cares?" she said. "Besides, you gave me the money I have in the first place. Besides, partners should share and share alike, right?"

"Right. Just don't mention me or Mary Kay to Higgins. He might try to back out if he knows three people are working on this."

"Not a word," she said. "I'm going to go seal the deal right now. But he's supposed to show me some building plans, and I really don't know much about that."

"Just make sure it's a wood-frame building, as large as the lot will take. And tell him you want two stories. But I really don't think you have to worry about it. He thinks he's going to own the building as soon as it's finished. I suspect he'll build well."

Sarah threw a wrap around herself and went bouncing out the door. I had to smile. There was money aplenty in Deadwood. I could name two dozen men rich enough to throw away five hundred dollars and never even miss it. But for the average miner, five hundred dollars was a year of panning.

For a girl Sarah's age, well, no one would ever think she could raise five hundred dollars in three months.

Might be we were taking advantage of Higgins by not telling him Sarah wasn't alone. On the other hand, his intent was to take advantage of her, so that evened it out. Even with three of us working on it, five hundred dollars was still a lot of money.

I sat down in a chair and Mary Kay came over and sat down gingerly on my lap. "Am I hurting your leg?" she asked.

"Even if you were," I said, "I'd never tell. You just stay right where you are."

CHAPTER 13

NEXT morning I went looking for a horse. The best deal that came my way was a strawberry roan with the look of a stayer in his build. The fellow who owned him was asking a hundred and sixty dollars, but I talked him down to one-forty, and had him throw in a saddle for ten more.

He wasn't Cap, but he wasn't bad, either. He already had the name Strawberry, and it seemed fitting, so I let it stand.

Most horses were geldings, but Strawberry was still a stallion and knew it. I rode him around a bit and he waited until he thought I wasn't ready, then went to bucking. For a couple of minutes it was nip and tuck, but he finally decided I knew a bit about riding. Knowing that, he just stopped bucking as sudden as he started.

I rode Strawberry back to the cabin and turned him loose in the corral. It was cold, and even with a bit of shelter I didn't like leaving him out like that. But I couldn't afford to keep him at the livery, and in truth, the cold really wouldn't bother him so long as he was well fed. But I made up my mind to put up a real stable as soon as time allowed.

Going inside the cabin, I threw together a proper outfit, then realized I didn't have a rifle. Mine was in the scabbard when Cap was stolen, and the need for another hadn't arisen. I thought about it and shrugged. After supper I'd walk down to Owen's cabin and get the loan of his.

Mary Kay is far and away the most beautiful woman I've ever seen. You can't name a thing about her that I don't think is perfect, whether it's her green eyes, her auburn hair, her lips, her figure, anything. But I tell you, if she was homely as a mud fence, I'd still have married her just for her cooking.

She put together a meal that night even better than usual, and that was saying something. Mary Kay was right when she said that Brennan was an eater, and he put away more than she did from that table.

It doesn't happen often, but when I was as full as it was possible to get, there was still food left on the table. It didn't seem right to stop eating while food still sat there in front of me, but for once I couldn't do anything about it. Mary Kay laughed. "I finally did it," she said. "I finally outcooked your stomach."

"Don't tell anyone about it," I said. "A thing like that could ruin a man's reputation."

"Don't worry," she said. "Even if I did tell, nobody would believe it."

Brennan, I noticed, still didn't have the hang of eating all the food he aimed at his mouth. About half of it made it past his lips; the rest of it he wore. Mary Kay cleaned him up, then sat him on the floor. Instead of pulling up and walking, he crawled into the living room. I lit a cigar and poured a cup of coffee.

Mary Kay cleaned off the table and started doing the dishes. Me, I sat there and watched her. It wasn't laziness on my part, really, it was just that of all the things she did around the cabin, washing dishes was the one thing I liked to just sit and watch . . . and listen to.

I can't think of anything that spells out home quite as plainly. The way she moved, the song she hummed softly to herself, the sound the dishes made clattering against each other. All of it somehow made me feel warm and comfortable and at home.

But after a time I stood up and stretched. "I'm going down to Owen's," I said. "Maybe I can walk off some of my supper."

"If you intend to walk off all you ate," Mary Kay said, "you'll still be walking when you hit Colorado."

I couldn't think of a single reply that wouldn't get me hit with a skillet, so I just grunted and let it pass. After belting my pistol around my waist, I slipped into my heavy coat, put on my hat, kissed Mary Kay on the neck, and stepped out the door.

I saw the flash of fire from the rifle only a split second before the bullet slammed into the door frame, showering me with splinters. The thunderclap of the shot shattered the stillness, but I was already moving. My momentum was carrying me out, so I jerked the door shut behind me and dived sideways into the shadows, drawing my Colt and thumbing back the hammer.

The rifleman was fifty or sixty yards away, and that's a long, long shot for a pistol. But I hoped I could at least come close enough to give him a scare. I waited for him to fire again.

His first shot had been aimed, and only the difficulty of seeing his sights in the night had saved me. Now he cut loose, firing rapidly, searching the front of the house with bullets. Aiming at the muzzle flash, I fired five times, as fast as I could thumb back the hammer, holding a little high because of the range.

I carried only five rounds in the Colt for safety, and after firing the last one I rolled over several times and went off the porch. There I stopped and reloaded by feel.

The cabin had gone dark almost as soon as the first shot was fired, and I knew Mary Kay had reacted in the right way, blowing out the lamps so the rifleman out there wouldn't have a target.

I wanted to go inside and see how she was doing, but I was afraid to risk it. Easing over to the window, I reached up and tapped it gently with my pistol, then whispered just loud enough for Mary Kay to hear if she was close. The windows all had glass in them, and that was something I took pride in. But a bullet had taken out the lower right-hand pane of glass in the window above me.

That scared me. It meant that at least one of the bullets had reached inside the cabin. But a moment later Mary Kay's voice floated out to me.

"We're all right," she said. "One of the bullets missed Brennan by inches, but he's fine. Is it safe now?"

"I don't know. The only way to be sure is to go out there and see. Take Brennan into one of the bedrooms and wait for me."

"All right," she said. "But be careful."

There was a full moon, but it was mostly covered by clouds. Now and then a gap in the clouds would let light through, and that made moving around a dangerous thing. A dark shape against the white snow might be mistaken for a boulder or a log, but if it was moving there could be little doubt it was a man. If I was caught in the open when the moon came out, I'd make a good target.

We'd had an easy winter so far, and while there was snow, it was no more than a foot deep most places. Here and there drifts piled up to three feet or so, but even that wasn't too bad. Waiting until the moon was fully hidden by clouds, I started off, intending to circle and come in on the unseen rifleman from another direction.

It was cold, and a soft wind from the north made it even colder. But twice on that stalk I had to change the Colt to my left hand for a moment to wipe sweat from my right palm. My stomach was tight and my heart beat slowly in my chest.

Deadwood was close enough for the shots to be heard, but far enough away that I doubted anyone would come to see what the ruckus was about, even if they heard. From the distance the shots might sound faint enough to ignore, though sound travels uncommonly well in the cold.

But I couldn't count on help from Deadwood. If anything was to be done, I had to do it myself.

I took my time. When the moon came out I froze wherever I happened to be, waiting for clouds before starting again. It was slow going, and when I moved at last into a position where I could see the spot where the rifleman had fired from, it was empty.

Had the man moved? Was he stalking me, or had he decided to quit after missing his first chance? The only way to tell was to circle the position and look for tracks. They weren't hard to find.

The tracks were of a man running, sometimes stumbling in his haste to get away. I followed them for fifty yards or so, and twice I found traces of blood on the snow. Not enough to come from a serious wound, but enough to let me know that the man was running away and not trying to set up a second ambush.

He would reach Deadwood well ahead of me, and following him was useless. Straightening up from the crouch I'd been in, I made my way back to the cabin. Before going inside I closed the wooden shutters on the windows, not wanting to chance being a target for a second time once the lamps were relit.

Mary Kay and Brennan were both all right. She showed me where Brennan had been standing, and I lined up the spot with the bullet that had crashed through the window. The bullet had missed Brennan by no more than three or four inches.

I've been angry before. I've been mad enough to charge hell with a bucket of water. But nothing in my life prepared me for the rage I felt when I realized how close my son had come to being killed.

Someone had robbed me, shot me, left me for dead. That no longer mattered. Someone had stolen Cap; that didn't matter either. What mattered was that someone had decided I was a danger and had to be killed, and had put my family in danger. Whoever it was had to be stopped before Mary Kay or Brennan was hurt.

Putting off my plan to see Owen for the night, I stayed with Mary Kay and Brennan until well after dawn. Sleep came hard, and several times I came awake without knowing why. Each time my eyes opened I lay for a time without moving, straining my ears into the darkness. Only when I was certain no one was out there did I go back to sleep.

Mary Kay was soft and warm beside me, and in the quiet I could hear Brennan breathing from across the room. It was a good sound. Snuggling close to Mary Kay under the cover, I put my arm around her and let my hand cup her breast. It was in that position I went to sleep.

CHAPTER 14

BRENNAN'S crying woke me up about dawn. I managed another half hour of sleep while Mary Kay nursed him, but then he started bouncing around on the bed, and on me, making more sleep impossible. Well, I thought, it's better than being woke up with a sharp stick. Not much, but some.

While Mary Kay made breakfast I went outside and looked around a bit, going to the spot where the shots had been fired from. There, only the tip of the barrel showing above the snow, I found a rifle. It was a '73 Winchester, and a good rifle . . . or it had been before the bullet from my Colt smashed into the action.

The bullet had done enough damage to make the rifle unusable, then had glanced off the metal, likely grazing whoever was holding the rifle. It had been pure luck on my part. Even in broad daylight I couldn't hit something at that range with a Colt very often. I'd gotten lucky, and when it comes to bullets, luck counts.

I went back to the cabin, washed up and shaved, then ate, my mind not on the food. Mary Kay was quiet, hardly speaking at all; only Brennan seemed unaffected by the previous night. When I finished the last of my food and drained my coffee cup, Mary Kay looked at me.

"You're still going after them, aren't you?" she asked.

I nodded. "There's no choice. As long as I'm alive, I'm a threat to the men who robbed me. Somehow I have to find them and stop them before they get lucky and kill me."

"Or one of us."

"Yes."

For a time she was silent. When she spoke again there was

anger in her voice. "Then find them," she said. "Find them and stop them. I don't want you to get killed, but at least you can defend yourself. Brennan can't. I've never wanted you to kill a man, but I'm beginning to understand how evil some men can be."

I stood up and went around the table. She came into my arms, and for a time we stood there. Then I kissed her, tasting the salt of a tear that ran down her cheek and onto her lips. It was the first time I could remember seeing her cry.

After a bit I went in search of Owen and found him still inside his cabin. He was using the cold weather as an excuse to stay inside and catch up on mending his tools and equipment. He greeted me at the door and invited me in, or at least I think he did. It was hard to understand exactly what he said, since his lips were closed around half a dozen small nails.

Once inside, I learned he was using the nails to fasten a new sole onto a pair of leather boots, and doing a fair country job of it. "When I was growing up," he said, "we made all the boots we wore. I never had a pair of store-bought boots until I was almost twenty."

I'd made a pair of boots once or twice, and several times I'd made moccasins, but I was nowhere near the cobbler Owen seemed to be. In less time than it takes to tell it, he had the sole in place.

"A pegged sole with stitches is best," he said. "But it also takes a lot more time. If I can get these boots through until spring I'll be happy."

Going to the stove, I took off the coffeepot and poured myself a cup. Then I sat down and told Owen about the night before. His brow was wrinkled with worry. "I'd like to say there ain't many men around mean enough to risk killing a baby while trying to kill a man," Owen said, "but in this town there's too many who don't give a damn.

"It could have been worse, though. You're lucky they didn't

toss a few sticks of dynamite through the window while you were asleep. Something like that happened down to Custer City a few weeks back."

Just the thought sent a wave of fear through me. Something like that would be difficult to stop, and unless you've seen how much damage a half dozen sticks of dynamite can do, you wouldn't believe it.

"Owen," I said, "I'm going out there and see if I can find Cap. He's the only lead I have to the men who robbed me, but I don't want to ride off and leave my family alone. It's a lot to ask, but I'd like you to move into my cabin while I'm away.

"There's two large bedrooms. Mary Kay and Sarah can share one, you can take the other. Odds are, once folks know I'm gone they won't try anything at the cabin, but you never know. Someone might get the idea of using Mary Kay and Brennan to get to me."

"Hell, Jim," Owen said. "I'd be glad to stay up there. Fact is, this place gets awfully lonely at times, and I could use a little home cooking.

"You go ahead and do what you have to do, and don't worry about your family. Anybody comes nosing around, I'll discourage them."

We talked a spell and I asked Owen about the use of his rifle. We decided he might need it while at my cabin, but we walked over to Henry Walsh's cabin and he loaned me his Winchester. It was a .44 caliber just like the one I'd had stolen, though with a longer barrel.

As we walked back to Owen's cabin he scratched at a two-day growth of beard on his chin. "Guess I'd best take a bath and shave before moving into your place," he said. "Living alone as I've been, it's almighty easy to let things like that slip by. Seems women take a dim view of it, though. Well, being around civilized people might do me good."

"You wouldn't be talking about Sarah, would you?" I asked. "She's pretty as a spring colt."

Owen blushed. "What makes you think that? I hadn't even noticed her. You say she's pretty?"

I snorted. "Hadn't noticed her? You can't take your eyes off her when she's around."

Owen grinned. "Well, maybe. I can't see anything coming of it, but it doesn't do any harm to dream a little."

Owen agreed to meet me at my cabin come first light, then went about finishing his boots. Me, I had a few things to do myself.

Not knowing when someone else might try to shoot me made worrying about money difficult, but I had to have it. It wasn't going to drop from the clouds, and it was just as unlikely I'd stumble across it by accident. The money I needed I would have to earn, and to earn it I would have to work. It was as simple as that.

First thing I did was stop by the sheriff's office. Seth Bullock was sitting behind his desk, shuffling a thick stack of papers. He nodded in greeting as I came through the door. "When I decided to become a lawman," he said, "I had visions of forming posses and riding after famous outlaws. Nobody told me about the paperwork."

"Might be I have something a bit more exciting for you to do," I said.

"Might be paperwork isn't so bad after all," he said. "But you may as well tell me about it."

I told him about the attack. "I wish you'd got a look at him," he said. "I'll take the rifle and show it around, and I'll check with all the doctors around town to see if one of them has patched a bullet wound in the last twelve hours or so, but I wouldn't count on finding the man too soon.

"But maybe we'll get lucky. You never know. Maybe he ran to a doctor and the doctor will remember him. Unless he's wounded worse than you think, though, he'll probably patch himself up or have a friend do it."

"That's about the way I see it," I said. "I've been on your side of the badge myself a time or two. Nothing ever comes easy."

"You got that right. But at least a good shooting breaks the routine. Last couple of weeks it's been mostly petty theft. Not a week goes by without some tenderfoot being cheated into thinking brass filings are gold dust. Sometimes I think they have it coming for being so gullible. But I have to spend time on every complaint."

"I can see where an old-fashioned murder might be a relief," I said. "Though I'd prefer the murder wasn't mine."

Bullock leaned forward a little and sighed. "Truth is," he said, "there does seem to be less serious trouble in town, but outside of town it's worse than ever."

We talked for a while about the criminal element, then about my plan to go after Cap. "I wish there were something I could do for you," he said, "but it's outside my jurisdiction. Usually I wouldn't let that stop me, but I'm afraid to leave Deadwood alone for that kind of trip.

"Technically, it won't be worth much out there, but I can swear you in and give you a badge. The army will honor it, and so will most town marshals and sheriffs. Thing is, you try to arrest someone and they put a bullet in you, a court would never convict them."

"Someone shoots me," I said, "and a court is the least of my worries. I'll take the badge, and thanks."

Bullock opened a drawer and took out a badge. He tossed it to me. "Raise your right hand," he said.

I raised my right hand. "Do you swear to uphold the law?" he asked.

"I do," I said.

"Then you are now a deputy sheriff. At least for however long it takes you to run down the lead on your horse."

I put the badge in my pocket, promised Sheriff Bullock I'd get the smashed rifle to him, then walked back up to the cabin. I was planning to leave at first light, and I wanted to spend as much time as possible with Mary Kay and Brennan before then.

CHAPTER 15

THE sun rises late when you're so far north and it's the dead of winter. I was up a good three hours before sunrise, and Mary Kay was up with me. Sarah was either still asleep or pretending to be so to give me and Mary Kay more time together.

We ate breakfast, then sat and talked quietly for a time. Most of our talk was about nothing in particular, and the one thing we took pains not to mention was the trouble I might be riding into. But I could see in Mary Kay's eyes that it was foremost in her mind. Not talking about it wouldn't make it go away, but it did keep it at arm's length.

About an hour before sunrise Owen showed up. He was carrying a rifle, a pistol, and enough ammunition to fight a war. He was also clean-shaven and dressed better than I'd ever seen him. He also smelled like a rose. I leaned closer and sniffed a little. Owen blushed.

"Had me a bath and a shave down to the barbershop," he said. "They splashed this smellgood on me before I could stop them."

"Since when do barbershops open this early?" I asked. "Seems to me you went to a lot of trouble just to watch over my cabin."

"No trouble at all," Owen said. "Not a barber in town who doesn't like to be roused early on a cold morning. Besides, if anyone should come calling while you're gone, I wouldn't want them to think they were in the company of a common ruffian."

About that time the door to Sarah's bedroom opened and she came out, wearing a nightgown with a thick robe over it.

Her hair was loose and her eyes were still full of sleep, but even I had to admit she was real fetching, all things taken into account.

Owen was wearing his hat, but the moment he saw Sarah he jerked it off his head and his face lit up. When Sarah saw Owen she blushed. She quickly turned away, her hands over her face.

"Oh," she said. "I didn't know anyone was here. I'm always such a mess when I get up in the morning."

"Miss Sarah," Owen said, "if you don't mind my saying so, I can't recall ever seeing anyone half so pretty, morning, noon, or night."

Sarah blushed deeper, the red starting at her throat and running quickly up into her cheeks. But even at that it was easy to see she was pleased. "Then you must have seen very few women early in the morning," she said. "I haven't done a thing with my face, and my hair is a mess."

"All that might be true," Owen said, "but you're still pretty as a spotted pony in a field full of wildflowers."

It came to Owen just what he was saying then, and he almost bolted for the door. "I . . . I forgot to, ah, check the corral and make sure everything's all right there," he said.

With that he was out the door. Me, I slipped into my coat and hat, then followed him out. When I caught up to him he was down by the corral, trying to roll a smoke with shaking hands. "Don't know what got into me," he said. "I never talked to a woman like that in my life. Reckon I made a fool of myself, and did a proper job of it."

It was cold, well below freezing, and I jammed my hands deep into the pockets of my coat. The cold was already seeping through my boots, and I stomped my feet a couple of times.

"Seems to me she liked it," I said. "I've never been much of a hand with women, but I imagine most of them can't help but like being told how pretty they are."

"You think so?"

I shrugged. "Like I said, I'm not much of a hand, but that's what Mary Kay tells me. Something else she told me once I've never forgotten. It's a line from a poem she read somewhere. I think it goes, 'Faint heart ne'er won a lady fair.' Makes sense when you think about it."

Owen thought a minute. "Meaning if a man wants to win himself a woman, he has to be bold?"

"That's the way it reads to me," I said. "Not that I know much about it."

Owen shook his head. "If that's true," he said, "I reckon I'm sunk. I'd sooner fight a bear with a switch than try to sweet-talk a woman."

"Seems to me you were doing pretty well in there," I said. "And speaking of in there, let's go back inside before my toes break off."

"Guess I'll have to face up to her sooner or later," Owen said. "Might as well get it over with."

We hadn't been out of the cabin more than fifteen minutes, but I noticed right away that Sarah had made the most of the time. She was wearing a green dress that brought out the color of her eyes, her hair was perfect, and she'd done something fine with her face. Owen looked at her and swallowed hard.

Mary Kay and Sarah were sitting at the table when we came in. They were leaning close to each other, obviously talking. Then they both looked up at Owen and giggled. Owen looked like he'd been hit between the eyes with an axe handle.

We sat down with a cup of coffee. "I've been thinking," I told Owen, "and Collin Driscoll's name keeps crossing my mind. There isn't a shred of evidence to suggest he's behind any of this, but he's the only man in Deadwood I've had words with. The odds are against it, but it might pay to keep an eye on him. Trouble is, I'm not sure how to go about it. I don't want you away from the cabin at night."

"He's a bad one, or so I'm told," Owen said. "I don't know

if keeping an eye on him would help or not, but it might give us a handle on who his friends are. Tell you what, work on the claims is almighty slow this time of year. Might be, Henry or one of the boys can do a little drinking down in the Badlands."

"I'd appreciate it," I said. "But tell them to go careful. If anyone gives them a hard time, tell them to forget it. Like as not, Driscoll doesn't have anything to do with it anyway."

"He still scares me," Sarah said. "Every once in a while I have to pass him on the street. You'd think he'd act angry, but he always smiles and tips his hat. Somehow that bothers me more than anything else he could do."

"How's that?" I asked.

Sarah shrugged and made a face. "I don't really know," she said. "He just doesn't act like you would expect him to. He reminds me of the cat who ate the canary."

"I think I see what you're getting at," I said. "It does seem like he'd be angry. He doesn't strike me as a man who would like losing."

There wasn't much left to say, so I went into the bedroom and started getting ready for my ride. First thing I did was slip into new long johns. They were extra thick and made of wool. Fact is, they itched a man near to death until he got used to them, but someone once said wool is warm and dry even when it's cold and wet. But I'd met more than one man who claimed it wasn't the wool that kept a man warm, it was all the moving you did scratching the itches.

I slipped on two pairs of socks, a cotton shirt, then a heavy wool shirt over that. I topped things off with a pair of homespun woolen pants, then pulled on my boots.

Brennan woke up about the time I pulled on the second boot, and I lifted him out of his bed. He rubbed at his eyes with the back of his hand. I kissed him on the cheek and carried him out into the kitchen. He was fine until he saw his mother, then he reached for her and began to cry.

"He always wants to nurse first thing," she said.

Mary Kay took Brennan into the other room to nurse him, and I used the time to get the last of my gear together. I was planning on traveling light and it didn't take long. All that remained was to saddle Strawberry, so I went to it. Me, I hated fighting a good horse, so I kept the saddle and everything else in a small room off the kitchen where the heat could reach it fairly well.

If a horse is broken properly he'll take a warm bit without trouble, but try forcing an ice cold bit in a horse's mouth and even the tamest of them will usually put up a fight. The saddle isn't as much trouble because there's a blanket between it and the horse, but I kept the saddle inside to protect the leather and for my own comfort. Last thing I wanted to do first thing in the morning was straddle a cold saddle.

Time I had Strawberry saddled and tied in front of the cabin, Mary Kay was finished nursing Brennan. We went into the bedroom for a minute to say goodbye in private. There really wasn't much to say, but I told her how much I loved her, then kissed her. For a time we stood holding each other, but at last we had to let go.

Mary Kay walked me to the door, and again we kissed, though little more than a peck this time. I hugged Mary Kay, then Brennan, shouted a "So long" to Owen and Sarah, then went out the door. After mounting Strawberry I turned away and rode down the hill.

A little later, when I was four or five hundred yards away, I turned and looked back toward the cabin. I could see smoke rising from the chimney, and memory of the warmth inside was still with me.

The windows were no more than tiny dots, but I raised a hand toward them. Then I turned Strawberry back down the trail. It suddenly seemed a lot colder than it had been only moments before.

CHAPTER 16

THE map Owen gave me was tucked into a pocket of my coat, but I'd long since memorized it and there was no need to pull it out. In good weather I figured the trip ahead of me would be no more than two or three days each way, but in the snow and cold I guessed it would take nearly twice as long.

I'd spent a good bit of time in cold weather over the years, though never quite so far north. But I knew how to live in the cold, and the trip wasn't at all bad once I got used to being out again.

Each night I built a small lean-to that blocked the wind and reflected the heat of a fire built in front. That was all I needed, and Strawberry needed even less. I'd camp each time at a spot where thick trees would keep him from the wind, and I made sure he got plenty of browse. We got along fine.

We reached the general area of the dugout not long before noon on the fourth day out of Deadwood. But it was only two hours before dark when I finally located the dugout itself. Dug into the hillside as it was, and covered with snow, it was nearly invisible. Only the door, a small window, and the chimney gave it away.

The corral was set to the right and back a bit from the cabin. It was sheltered from the wind by a rise in the land on two sides, and a crudely built, low stable occupied another side. The shelter looked large enough for only half the horses in the corral, and that meant only the best horses would be inside.

The snow in front of the dugout was well trampled, with

one obvious path leading to the stable and a second going down to a stream fifty yards away. An inch or so of snow had fallen the night before, and the new snow made it easy to tell which tracks had been made since morning.

Unfortunately, it also erased any tracks made earlier. I was a hundred yards away, standing in the shelter of some brush and low pines, and from that distance the tracks in the snow were a confused muddle.

I'd hoped to simply ride up and see Cap in the corral, go to the door of the cabin and flash my badge, then arrest Denny and his partner. That was what I hoped, but I knew it wasn't going to be that easy.

To begin with, I could barely see the corral, but I was pretty sure Cap wasn't in it. If he was there at all, it was inside the stable. I'd have to get a lot closer before there would be any chance at all of getting a look inside the stable, but it was the only way to be sure.

Pulling back another two hundred yards, I found a spot where most of the area around the dugout was no longer visible, but the door itself could still be seen. Then I waited.

Half an hour later a man came out the door, carrying a wooden bucket. He walked down to the stream and dipped a bucketful of water and carried it back. It has to get almighty cold to freeze a fast-flowing stream like that one, and when it does freeze it's from the bottom up. If I was any judge, that stream would have at least a little water flowing all winter along.

That was a rawhide outfit down there, and no doubt about it, they'd picked a good location for lasting out the winter.

A little later a second man made three trips outside, each to gather an armload of wood from a stack near the left corner of the dugout.

Then darkness came, light filled the window of the dugout, and the cold began to work its way through me. But I huddled down without a fire and waited almost two hours, shivering all the while. When I could take it no longer, I stood up, stomped life back into my legs, and began walking a wide circle around the dugout.

Only the gentlest of breezes was blowing, but I took care to approach the stable from downwind. Once there, I opened the crude door slowly and stepped inside. The stable was out of sight of the dugout, so I took a chance and struck a match. Cupping it in my hands to prevent a draft from blowing out the flame, I looked around.

The stable was some larger than it had seemed from my position on the hill, and it held seven horses. But Cap wasn't there. Nor was there a horse that came close to resembling Cap. Easing back to the door, I blew out the match and stood in the darkness.

Too many possibilities filled my mind. It was possible that Cap had been in the corral and was now gone. It was possible Cap had never been there at all. It was possible the man who told Owen about the dugout was simply making up the story, or had been mistaken.

It was also entirely possible I'd strayed off the route laid out in the map and had found the wrong dugout. Such places were not uncommon, and if I was even a little off in my reckoning, I could easily have missed the place I was searching for.

One thing was certain . . . not finding Cap in the stable left me in a quandary. In fact, it left me with only three options that made sense. I could quit and head back to Deadwood, I could camp out in the surrounding hills and watch the dugout for a few days in case Cap showed up, or I could knock on the door of the dugout and see what the men inside had to say.

I wasn't yet ready to concede defeat, so going back to Deadwood was out of the question. I briefly considered watching the dugout for a few days, then dismissed that idea as well. The cold did not frighten me, but it was simply too risky. Unless it snowed or the wind blew much harder than it was now blowing, come morning those men would find my tracks going in and out of the stable.

And even if snow or wind did conceal my tracks, there was still a chance I'd be spotted. Those men had to know the surrounding country much better than I did, and anything out of place, even a man's face showing two hundred yards away, might be spotted.

That left the third option. I wasn't looking forward to it, but on the other hand, I was already half-convinced Cap had never been here and the men inside had nothing to do with my ambush.

Circling back around to Strawberry, I stepped into the saddle and rode down to the dugout. Knocking on the door had been a figure of speech, and not something I planned to do at all. Stopping Strawberry thirty yards short of the dugout, I called loudly, "Hello the dugout."

No more than thirty seconds later the door opened a bit and a rifle barrel came through. Behind the rifle barrel was a man's face. "Who's out there?" the man yelled. "And what do you want?"

I said the first thing that came to mind. "Name's Jim Miller," I said. "I'm hunting shelter for the night, and hot coffee if you have it."

For a full minute the man said nothing, then yelled to me again. "Come on in, an' do it with your hands empty."

I rode Strawberry up to the dugout and climbed from the saddle. There was a hitch rail off to the side a bit and I looped the reins about it. Walking up to the door of the dugout, I stomped my feet a couple of times. The man was still standing there. The door was open wider, but the rifle was still in his hands. As I approached he stepped aside to let me in.

The dugout was one room, maybe ten by twelve feet. The ceiling was just high enough so that I could stand erect with two inches or so to spare. There was a small table, four chairs, and a wood-burning stove. In one corner a board had been fastened to the wall for a shelf. On it sat a water bucket and a washbasin.

The floor was made of split logs, rounded side down. Blankets covered the floor of the side away from the stove, and I knew that's where the men slept. The corner of the room nearest the blankets was piled high with saddles and other gear, none of it organized.

The only light came from a kerosene lamp in the middle of the table, but it was enough to see that the place was filthy. Now, there's just no way to make a place like that spotless, but these men never even tried.

The man who let me into the dugout was tall, but bony and a little stoop-shouldered. His hair was thinning badly and he wore a long, handlebar mustache. He was wearing striped pants, no shirt, but had his suspenders over his long underwear.

A second man sat at the table and I looked him over. He was no more than five-nine or so, but he had a stocky build. His shirtsleeves were rolled up to the elbow and thick muscles pushed outward every time he raised his coffee cup to his mouth.

He had sandy brown hair. A stubble of beard showed against the tan of his face, and his black eyes were cold and hard. He was wearing a pistol belt. A bowie knife with a twelve-inch blade hung on his left side. There was nothing friendly in his face. I decided I didn't care.

The man who let me in closed the door and sat his rifle so it leaned against the door frame. "I'm Olsen Toliver," he said. "That's Solomon Smith. What was it you said your name was?"

"Jim Miller. Most folks call me Colorado. It was friendly of you all to let me in. I thought I was going to have to spend another night curled up in the snow."

"Not much room here," Toliver said, "but we'll make do if you don't mind sleeping on a hardwood floor?"

"I've slept in places that make this look like a first-class hotel," I said truthfully. "That coffee sure smells good."

"There's cups by the water bucket," Toliver said. "He'p yourself."

The dugout was hot, and it was thick with the smell of unwashed bodies and concentrated tobacco smoke. Taking off my coat, I hung it on the back of a chair, poured myself a cup of coffee, and sat down. The man named Smith still hadn't spoken, but he was staring at me hard.

"The name don't ring any bells," he said, "but I could swear I've seen you somewhere."

"Could be," I said. "I've been there."

"You've been where?"

"Somewhere," I said. "I've been somewhere."

He wasn't sure whether or not I was trying to be smart. "What do you mean by that?"

"Why, nothing at all," I said. "Just that I'm a well-traveled man, and you have the look of travel about you. Might be we've crossed trails somewhere."

That calmed him down. "Yeah, I see your point," he said, "but I'm usually pretty good with names. I can't recall ever hearing yours."

"Hell," Toliver said, "I knew a man for better than five years once, and every time I saw him he called himself by a different name. Out here many a man changes his name more often than he changes his shirt."

"Now that I can believe," Smith said. "Time or two I've used another handle myself."

Up until I decided to come into the dugout I'd been wearing the badge Sheriff Bullock gave me, but now it was tucked deep into a pocket of my coat. Smith was talking more now, but he never took his eyes off me, and it was almost like he could smell the badge.

Toliver seemed friendlier, but even he kept a short-barreled Remington tucked into his pants. I'd seen too many men on both sides of the law not to know the difference.

These two might have had nothing to do with ambushing me, but they were far from innocent ranchers. My bet was they were horse thieves. Small-time thieves, at that.

The area east of the Black Hills was good grassland, and a number of legitimate ranchers had moved onto it, but this outfit didn't shape up that way. A man intending to ranch in this country might live in a dugout for a year or two, but he would never try raising cattle or horses without putting up hay for the winter.

Nor would he spend a winter out like this with no more horses than these two had. It simply wasn't worth it. Not one of those horses was worth anything when it came to breeding, and not one of them would be worth a penny more when spring came. It made me wish I'd checked the brands.

I was willing to bet I'd either find a wide range of brands, or a single brand used to cover all the old ones.

But even if I was right about that, it proved nothing. What I needed was something that would either tie these men directly to the ambush or prove they had nothing to do with it. But how to do it? All that came to mind was talking to them, hoping one of them would slip and say something I could use.

Time and coffee loosens most men's mouths, and these two were no exception . . . up to a point. After a time we got around to talking about the horses they had.

"Odd time of the year to be holding horses like those," I said. "Why not sell them off and buy better when spring comes?"

"Hell," Smith said. "You haven't even seen them. What makes you think they ain't worth keeping?"

That's when I took a chance. "I've seen them," I said. "Before I rode in here and hailed the cabin I had a look around, including inside the stable."

Smith's face went hard. "You were inside the stable? What gave you the right to do that?"

I smiled. "It wasn't a matter of right," I said. "When a man rides trails by night, he'd be a fool to come up on a place like this without having some kind of idea about who's inside."

Toliver shifted a little so his hand was nearer his pistol. "But you came on in," he asked. "You're no fool, and you sure act like you got us pegged. But you still came in?"

"Why not come in?" I asked. "Sure, as soon as I got a good look at those horses I knew they were likely stolen. This isn't a working ranch, and you don't hold geldings for breeding stock. Those horses are still out there because you have to be careful where you try to sell them."

"If you figured out that much," Smith said, "why'd you come inside?"

"Seemed like the safest place to spend the night," I said. "Like I said, when you ride trails by night, you have to be careful. All I wanted to know when I checked the stable was how many men were likely in here. But finding those horses made me feel right at home."

"You saying you've stole horses?"

"Never stole a horse in my life," I said. "Cattle, now that's another story. Mostly I do whatever it takes to get the coon. Look at it this way, why else would I come inside unless I was telling the truth?"

"You might be the law," Toliver said.

"If that was the case," I said, "you'd both be dead or on your way back to jail by now. Trouble with a dugout is that you can't guard the back. If I was the law I would have waited until morning, then circled around, climbed over the back side of the hill, and walked right down to your roof.

"Sooner or later you'd have walked out and I'd have had you dead to rights. Of course, a man up there could kick the stovepipe off and smoke you out if he didn't like waiting. Or even cave the roof in, for that matter. You've got what, two feet of sod over a layer of poles? No, if I was the law, I wouldn't have need to come in."

Toliver looked at Smith. "He's got a point there. This place is mighty comfortable, but there ain't no way to defend it proper."

"Besides," I added. "Far as I know, only the army has jurisdiction out here. A lawdog would have to be a fool to come way out here looking for trouble."

"That's true enough," Smith said. "But every now and then one of them tries it anyway. But you got one point—wouldn't no lawman come in the way you did."

It seemed both of them believed me well enough. Slowly they came to accept me as a man who wore the same stripe they did. You couldn't say Solomon Smith really warmed up, but he struck me as a man who would be the same whether talking to a friend or to an enemy. He just wasn't the friendly type.

After a couple of hours we gave up talking and I went outside long enough to unsaddle Strawberry and put him in the corral. The cold air actually felt good after the stuffiness of the dugout.

Back inside, I took time to spread my blankets on the floor. "You just barely have enough room here for two," I said. "Might be a little close having three of us sleeping here."

"Huh," Toliver grunted. "You should stick around a spell. Most nights there's only two of us here, but we've a partner who comes in once a week or so. Three's no problem.

"You want to see it cramped, come some night when there's eight or ten men stretched out on the floor. It don't happen often, but you never know from one week to the next who Denny will bring in with him."

When Toliver said the name *Denny*, my heart jumped into my throat. My surprise must have shown on my face as well, because he looked at me funny. "What's wrong with you?" he asked. "You know Denny?"

I thought fast. "I know a man named Denny," I said. "Thomas Denny. Skinny snake with a scar running across his nose and down his cheek."

"Naw," Toliver said. "Wrong Denny. Estle Denny is a big man. As tall as you and twenty pounds or more heavier. That other Denny you mentioned, he a friend?"

"Not hardly," I said. "The weasel got drunk one night and tried to shoot me. That's how he got the scar."

"Denny should be back sometime tomorrow," Toliver said. "If you're still around, you can meet him. He might even put you to work, if you're in the market to make some money."

"I'm always in the market for money," I said. "What would I have to do?"

"You picky?" Smith asked.

"Only in the risks I have to take," I said. "If there's a chance of being shot at, my asking price goes up."

"In this business there's always a chance of getting shot at," Smith said. "Does that scare you?"

"I've been shot at," I said, "and yeah, it scares me. It scares me so bad I usually have to shoot back to calm my nerves."

Toliver looked me up and down. "You wear that six-gun like a man who knows how to use it," he said. "If you're good, really good, that'll score high with Denny. He says the hardest thing to find is a man who's really as fast with a gun as he claims."

"What's being fast have to do with stealing horses?" I asked. "Unless he does things different, most of that work is done at night."

"Stealing horses ain't all Denny has going," Toliver said. "The boss has Denny doing all kinds of things. Why—"

"Shut up, Toliver," Smith said. "You talk too much."

"What's the matter with you?" Toliver asked him. "Miller will probably be working with us after tomorrow. You know how hard Denny looks around for people who can use a gun?"

"We don't know he can use a gun," Smith said. "Might be he'd shoot off his own toe if he tried to draw fast. If Denny hires him, then he can tell him what he wants him to know. Until then, just shut up."

"Have it your way," Toliver said. "Guess it's time we all got some sleep anyway."

"That's the smartest thing I've heard tonight," I said. "It's been a long day and I could use some rest."

Smith threw several chunks of wood into the stove, then blew out the lamp. For a long time after, I looked up at the ceiling, trying to plan how I would handle the next day. Nothing useful came to mind. All I could do was wait and see how things developed.

A lot would depend on whether Denny came in alone or brought friends with him. It also depended on whether or not he recognized me. I usually wore a trimmed mustache, but now I had a four-day growth of beard to go along with it. Was that enough to keep him from knowing me?

For that matter, did he even know what I looked like up close? It could well be he'd never seen me except over the sights of a rifle.

What complicated things was the way Toliver had mentioned Denny having a boss. If that was true, then it was the boss I wanted. If I could find out who he was, I stood a chance of getting at least a part of my money back. An outside chance, maybe, but still a chance.

Yet as I lay there looking up at the ceiling, the thought came to me that it still wasn't too late to walk away from the whole thing. All I had to do was get up and leave as soon as it was light. Mary Kay would be waiting, and so would Brennan.

Then I sighed. It wouldn't work. Even if I rode away they wouldn't believe I'd quit. Out here no one had recognized me so far, but in Deadwood I was known on sight. Whoever tried to kill me once would try again.

No, it had to end. I couldn't risk putting my family in the path of a bullet for a second time. Once the name of Denny was mentioned I was convinced I'd found the right bunch. And now that I knew who they were, I had to stop them. It had to end once and for all.

CHAPTER 17

MORNING came all too soon. Unable to sleep any longer, I was the first to crawl out of my blankets. My back was stiff and my neck hurt from sleeping on the floor, but I figured getting up and moving around was the best thing for it.

The fire in the stove was nearly out, but the dugout was well insulated by the surrounding earth, and it was still warm. After throwing a bit of wood into the stove to get a fire going, I slipped into my boots, put on my coat, and went outside.

The cold air felt good after a night in the stuffy dugout, and I took my time checking on Strawberry. Giving him a bit of grain I found in the stable, I patted his neck and went back outside. Going to the stream, I knelt in the snow and drank deeply of the ice-cold water. It tasted wonderful.

Lighting a cigar, I sat down on a rock near the dugout and watched the sun finally clear the horizon. Only then did I go back inside the dugout. Toliver was up already, looking bleary eyed, but working at the stove to fix a breakfast of salt pork and beans.

Smith was still in his blankets, but sitting up and rolling a smoke. He struck a match with his thumbnail and lit the cigarette, inhaled deeply, coughed. "I hope Denny brings a couple of replacements," he said. "I'm getting damn tired of this place. I'd give a double eagle for a soft bed and a good meal."

"I'd give a double eagle for a woman," Toliver said. "And I wouldn't be any too particular about what woman it was, neither."

"What time you figure Denny will get in?" I asked.

"No telling," Toliver said. "He's supposed to ride in sometime today, but you never can tell. Why, did you decide to wait for him?"

I shrugged. "Maybe. If he doesn't take too long getting here. I could use some easy money, but I don't aim to sit around too long waiting."

"Don't get the wrong idea," Smith said. "There's nothing easy about working for Denny. Half the time you're stuck in some hole like this, an' the other half you're riding long, cold trails by night, or somebody is trying to part your hair with a bullet."

From time to time I'd heard folks talk about being an outlaw as though it were a glamorous, romantic thing. Anybody who believed that should have spent a night with Solomon Smith and Olsen Toliver. I knew dirt poor farmers who lived better.

We ate a greasy breakfast, then went about taking care of the morning chores. Chopping wood was one chore, feeding and currying the horses was another. Wanting to keep on the good side of Toliver and Smith, I pitched in and lent a hand.

Besides, I've always been a working man, and when there's something to be done I like to get at it.

Neither Toliver or Smith seemed overanxious to tackle the wood pile, so I picked up the axe and went to work. That's something else I've noticed about outlaws . . . most of them shy away from hard work. No matter, using an axe was something I'd always enjoyed. I like the way it feels to swing an axe, and to split a chunk of dry wood.

Splitting wood isn't the hardest thing in the world, but it isn't as easy as it looks, either. If you drive the blade of the axe straight down into the wood you might split it, but you might also get the blade stuck in the wood and have to waste time pulling it loose. The trick is to twist the blade just a touch as it strikes the wood. The wood splits easier, and the blade doesn't get stuck.

It was a cold morning, but swinging an axe uses a lot of

energy. It wasn't long before I took off my coat, then my heavy outer shirt.

Toliver and Smith were out at the stable taking care of the horses—that's something any outlaw will take pains to do. If you have to run from a posse a good, grain-fed horse can mean the difference between getting away or hanging. I was still swinging the axe when they returned.

Toliver looked at the wood I'd split and whistled. "Hell, man," he said. "We usually just split enough for the day. You've already split enough to last a cold week."

"Grew up swinging an axe," I said. "Guess I got a little bit carried away."

"You can get carried away like that any time you want," Smith said. "If there's one thing I can't abide, it's swinging an axe."

With the horses cared for and the wood chopped, there was very little left to kill time. Toliver brought out a deck of worn cards and for a time we played poker for small change. I made it a point to lose a few dollars. "If we could keep you around for a time," Toliver said, "we might not have to steal any more horses."

It was two in the afternoon when Estle Denny came riding in. He didn't come alone. Two men were with him, and both had the look of outlaws. The poker game was over and I was sitting in front of the cabin again, shivering a little, but glad to be in the open air. When I saw the riders coming I slipped the thong off my Colt. My heart was beating faster, and I knew if Denny recognized me, all hell was going to break loose.

Opening the door of the dugout, I called inside that riders were coming. Toliver and Smith both came to the door.

"It's Denny," Smith said. "Looks like he brought our relief along with him."

Moving over to a spot where my back was against the dugout wall, I watched the men come. A big man wearing black pants and a gray hat was leading. His eyes locked on me a hundred yards out. They never left me even when he reined in and slid from the saddle. "Who the hell are you?" he asked.

"They call me Colorado," I said. "I drifted in last night. Toliver said you might be able to use a man who was good with a gun, so I stuck around."

He looked at my face closely. "Damn if you don't look familiar," he said. "You been around these parts long?"

"Nobody's been around these hills long," I said. "Fact is, I drifted in a couple of months back."

"Where were you before that?"

"Cheyenne," I said. "Denver, El Paso, Taos, you name it and I've likely been there."

"You really good with a gun?"

"I get by."

Denny smiled. "You don't mind if I test you on that, do you?" he asked. "Anybody can say they're good."

Smith and Toliver were both in front of the dugout now, and all five of them were watching me. Most likely they were curious, wanting to see just how good I was. If I could back up my talk Denny would probably hire me. If I couldn't, he would tell me to ride . . . or put a bullet in me.

I shrugged. "However you want it. But you might not like the answer."

Denny pulled back in mock fear. "Now you got me scared," he said. "Maybe I better test you on a target."

He called the two new men over. Both were slender, medium-tall men. One had long, greasy brown hair and prominent front teeth. The other wore his hair short and might have been handsome had someone not sliced off part of his lip.

"Meet Harvey Segal and Johnny Blavins," Denny said. "Harvey is pretty fair with a six-gun himself. You wouldn't mind going up against him—in a little target shooting, that is?"

"Sure," I said. "Why not?"

Denny smiled and spoke to the other man, the one named Blavins. "Take half a dozen sticks o' that firewood and set them up out there a piece," he said. "We'll see how good this gent really is."

Blavins loaded up with wood and paced off twenty-five yards. There he set the firewood in the snow. He grouped the firewood so each of us had three targets, then he walked back to where we stood.

The pieces of firewood were two feet long and maybe six inches wide, but he'd jammed them deep in the snow and a little less than half of them showed. A good shot could hit them, an average shot couldn't. Then again, most men couldn't hit a bull in the butt from ten feet with a handgun.

"How do you want it?" Denny asked. "Aim and fire, or from the draw?"

I shrugged. "From the draw, then," he said. "First man to hit all three targets wins."

Harvey Segal faced his targets and I faced mine. We were ten feet apart and I took a minute to size him up. He was skinny, dirty, and had front teeth like a squirrel—but he wore a Colt like he knew how to use it.

He wore a glove on his left hand, but none of his right, and the hand was tanned and weathered from exposure to rain and wind and sun. The butt of his Colt was worn smooth by frequent usage, and that meant he was probably pretty good. Just how good remained to be seen.

Denny stood behind us. "When I clap my hands," he said, "both of you draw."

My feet were a little apart, my arm and hand loose by my side. I was breathing shallow and concentrating on the targets. "Want to make it more interesting?" Denny asked.

I looked back at him. "What did you have in mind?"

"I've got a double eagle that says Harvey beats you. Unless you're afraid to bet?"

I needed to win, and I needed to show Denny I would fit in with his outfit. It was the best chance I had to learn who his boss was. "I don't have a double eagle," I said. "But I do have a strawberry roan in the stable that's worth an easy one-fifty. Will you put up a hundred dollars against him?"

Denny whistled. "You must be pretty confident," he said. "What the hell, it's a bet. I've only seen one man who's better with a gun than Harvey."

I faced the targets again. "Get ready," Denny said.

The seconds ticked by, and after a minute or so Denny suddenly slapped his hands together. I drew and fired three times, the shots coming so close together they sounded almost like one.

Two of the targets flipped backward out of the snow, and the third, hit right on the edge, spun crazily and dropped. I looked over at Harvey. His gun was out and cocked but he hadn't fired a shot. His face was a mixture of surprise and anger. "Luck," he said. "Pure damn luck."

Denny laughed. "Yeah," he said to Harvey. "Lucky he wasn't shooting at you." Then he told me, "Looks like I owe you a hundred. I would take a crack at you myself, but I might lose another hundred."

"You *might*?"

He stepped up beside me. "See Harvey's targets?" he asked. I nodded.

He drew and fired three times, every bit as fast as I had. All three targets flipped backward. "Yeah," he said. "I *might*."

Toliver put up their horses while the rest of us went into the dugout and emptied the coffeepot. There weren't enough chairs to go around, but Solomon Smith went out to give Toliver a hand. Denny sipped his coffee and began rolling a smoke. "I doubt there's a dozen men in the country as fast or as accurate as you," he said. "Seems like I should have heard your name."

"I could say the same for you," I said. "I can't recall ever hearing of anyone named Estle Denny.

"Anyway, it's mostly a matter of luck," I added. "There's a

lot of men around who can use a gun, and use it well. But if they stay away from trouble you never hear about them."

"That may be," he said, "but I've never seen anyone better than you . . . unless it's me."

"Wild Bill was better," I said. "I once saw him split five out of five playing cards at twenty yards. Best I ever did was three out of five."

"He was really that good?"

"He was," I said. "And he claimed Jim Courtright was as good or better."

We talked for a spell, and I found myself liking Estle Denny. He was a hard man and on the wrong side of the law, but he had a pleasant way of talking. Yet I was pretty certain he was one of the men who ambushed me and stole Cap. I kept that in mind as we talked.

"If you're still looking for a job," he said, "I'll give you a try. You'll go along on a couple of small jobs first, and if they work out, I'll do right by you."

"Thanks," I said. "I could sure use some money about now."

"Ah, that reminds me. I owe you a hundred for beating Harvey."

Denny took a leather pouch from his vest pocket and counted out five double eagles. He bounced them around in his hand a couple of times, listening to the clinking sounds of the heavy coins slapping together. Then he spread them out in front of me on the table. I scooped them up and slipped them into my pocket.

"Thanks," I said. "I think I could get to like working for you."

"It won't always be this easy," Denny said. "Fact is, I know just how to start you off. Me and the boys here just took a dozen head of horses south and sold them. Fellow said the army is going to be buying in Cheyenne next month, so we need a nice herd to give them.

"There's a rancher north and east of here who raises the

best horseflesh around. Zach Watson is his name, and I think he's ripe to pick. If you work out on this job we'll see about taking you on something bigger."

I was playing everything by ear. Breaking the law was something I had no intention of doing, but I had to stretch out the string as far as possible. "Sounds good," I said. "Especially the bigger job later on. If I'm off-base with this just say so, but I'm told you have a boss yourself. Mind if I ask who it is?"

"No, I don't mind at all," Denny said. "I won't tell you, but you can ask. Had to be Toliver mentioned the boss, I reckon. His mouth is going to get him killed."

I lit a cigar and took a drink of coffee. "Don't make me no nevermind," I said. "Just like to know who's paying my tab, is all."

"I'd worry if you didn't, but this time you'll have to take me as boss. I'm the only one who knows who the boss is, and it has to stay that way. If you can't work like that you're free to ride."

"Reckon I'll stick," I said. "Guess there is one thing I should tell you, though."

"What's that?"

"If you have any jobs in Deadwood you'll have to count me out. The sheriff there knows me, and he'd give a lot to see me in jail."

"On what charge?"

"Armed robbery. Seems he thinks I held up a miner last week."

"Did you do it?"

"Yeah. But all I got was about thirty dollars. Sure thought he'd be carrying more than that."

Denny laughed. "That's why you need me," he said. "We never leave anything to chance. Before we do a job we know to the penny how much we'll get."

I drained the coffee cup and stood up. "Sounds good to

me," I said. "I don't know about spending much time in this place, though. When do you plan to go for the horses?"

"As soon as it looks like snow," Denny said. "No point in leaving an easy trail to follow. Might be tonight, might be two weeks. No telling."

"Well," I said. "I guess I can stand if it you can. But right now I'm going out and try to get a shot at something worth eating. Not much here but salt pork and beans, and it doesn't look like you brought anything better."

"Never gave it a thought," Denny said. "Usually we rustle up a stray cow or the like. And I didn't figure on being here any longer than necessary.

"And we usually don't like showing ourselves around the country any more than necessary. But it might not be a bad idea at that. Take Blavins with you. He's a fair hand with a rifle and knows the country."

He wasn't really giving me a choice—Denny didn't know me well enough to trust me yet, and that was to be expected. But I didn't mind. Mostly I just wanted to get out of the dugout for a spell. And truth to tell, some fresh meat would go down well.

So I saddled Strawberry and rode out with Blavins. He wasn't much on talking, but that was fine. It gave me a chance to think.

I had no idea how to handle the situation. There were five men at the dugout now, and that was more than I wanted to handle. There seemed little chance of prying the name of the boss from Denny, at least while he was out here, so what was the right course of action? One thing was certain, Denny would talk only if he had to, and he didn't have to while he was free.

Somehow I had to cut him from the bunch and take him back to Deadwood. Maybe there the pressure on him would be enough to make him talk. But getting him alone for a time wasn't going to be easy. All I could really do was keep my eyes open and grab the chance when and if it came.

I was so wrapped up in my own thoughts that I didn't see the elk until after Blavins fired. His bullet caught the elk through the lungs and it bolted, but we both fired again and it went down, throwing up a spray of snow. Johnny Blavins was even better with a knife than with a rifle, and between us we had the elk skinned in short order.

There was too much meat to carry, but we took all we could and hung the rest in a tree for later retrieval. When we got back to the dugout another poker game was in progress, and I joined in. From that moment on, it became a waiting game.

CHAPTER 18

IT was eight days before Denny thought the weather right for the raid on Zach Watson's horses. By that time I was getting so restless it was hard to sit still. Yet I had no real idea how I was going to get Denny back to Deadwood.

In the first place, he was almighty good with a gun. And even if I was faster, it didn't matter, because I didn't want to kill him. He was no good to me dead. Somehow I had to separate him from the others, and then do what I could.

When he announced the time for the job had come, I hoped my chance had also. One thing I'll say for him, he knew how to go about his business. The snow already on the ground had been softened and packed tight by the sun, and only a damn fool would try stealing horses under those conditions. It would be far too easy for a group of angry cowboys to track the horses.

Then, on the eighth day, the sky closed in with low, gray clouds, and snow began to fall. Denny stepped outside and looked up at the sky. "It's now or never," he said. "This snow looks like it'll last a time. Should cover our tracks fine if we can get a head start."

He came back inside and called us together. He drew a map of the country where the horses were kept, sketching in buildings and landmarks. "The herd is no more than a half mile from the ranch house," he said. "That means no shooting. Watson usually has a couple of men keeping an eye on the horses, but we should be able to handle them without trouble."

"What if we can't?" Segal asked.

"Then we wait until we can, or we pass on the job," Denny

said. "Watson has better than a dozen men working for him, and this time of the year most of them will be close to the ranch house, probably in the bunkhouse. They're tough men, and I don't want them too close behind us."

"Where do we drive the horses once we get them started?" I asked. "That's pretty open country around there, isn't it?"

"Not as open as a man would think," he said. "It's full of draws and the like, but we ain't stopping for anything. Once we get the horses we move them south and keep moving them, come hell or high water.

"Toliver, you can stay here and keep an eye on things while we're gone. That might be a week, or it might be a month. You just sit tight."

"Ah, hell," Toliver said. "I already been cooped up in this rat hole forever. Why can't one of the new men stay?"

"I'll stay here," Blavins said. "I'm a warm-weather body myself. You all go right ahead and take your time. Me, I'll sit here with a warm fire and a full belly."

"All right," Denny said. "It's settled then. Everybody saddle up. We might as well pull our stakes before the weather closes us down."

We saddled our horses, packed a few things, and started off. Most of us had a bit of jerky tucked away in our saddlebags, a handy thing to have in cold weather, and I took a piece out and chewed on it as we rode. It was frozen solid, and even when it thawed in my mouth it was like chewing leather.

I was still playing it by ear, but I knew the one thing I couldn't do was let Denny and his men steal the horse herd. I wasn't going to be involved in stealing horses, but four of them and one of me didn't stack up to good odds.

We rode most of the night and camped on a spot of high ground, building only a tiny fire that gave us coffee and light, but no real food. After clearing a spot in the snow, I curled up in my blankets and slept reasonably well. Cold as it was, it was better than the dugout.

When morning arrived Denny led us on foot to a spot where we could look out over a large section of country. He pointed to the northeast. "That's Watson's ranch," he said. "If you look close you can see the horses in that wide draw. You can even see smoke rising from the chimney of the house.

"There's really nothing keeping the horses together except a couple of guards and the fact that Watson keeps hay and grain out for them."

"What guards?" Segal asked. "I can barely see the horses from here, let alone men."

"I spent a month working for Watson," Denny said, "and he's a tough boss, but a fair one. He doesn't ask his men to do anything he wouldn't do himself, so he doesn't try to make them ride guard on the herd when the weather gets this bad.

"You can't see it from here, but there's a small shack that overlooks the horse herd. In hard weather the guards stay there. It ain't the most comfortable place to spend a night, but it has a small stove and keeps the wind off. Two men with rifles there could stand off half the Sioux Nation."

"So how do we get to the horses?" I asked. "Those men see us and they'll cut loose."

"It's going to be a dark night," Denny said. "They won't be able to see much of anything from the shack. But you're right, we can't take the chance. Seems to me the best thing we can do is ride up there and get the drop on them."

"Just like that," Smith said. "We ride up the hill pretty as you please and ask them to drop their guns?"

Denny smiled. "Something like that. Those men will be watching for anything out of the ordinary. Try sneaking up on them and they'll see us sure. But if a couple of us ride around and come in from the direction of the ranch, talking and laughing like a couple of regular hands?"

"Then the men inside the cabin won't spook," I said.

Denny nodded. "They won't know why we're coming, but

they're bound to think we're friends. We shouldn't have any trouble with them if we do it right."

"Which two ride to the guard shack?" I asked.

"Figured me and Segal would," Denny said. "Why?"

"No real reason," I said. "Just wondering what would happen if things go wrong. Might be best to have the fastest guns where the shooting is likely to be."

"Meaning you want to ride along with me? That's not such a bad idea."

Denny pointed out other features of the terrain and explained what each man's job was. While the two of us took out the guards, Segal, Smith, and Toliver would move down and slowly start the horses moving south. If everything went right, the horses would be ten miles away come daylight, and the falling snow would wipe out all or most of the tracks.

"One last thing," Denny said. "Those horses are worth a lot of money, and I mean to have them. But not at the price of going to jail. There's to be no shooting. If anything goes wrong, if you hear a single shot, forget the horses and ride like hell. We'll meet right here. There's always another job."

That was the way we left it. Going back to the fire, we settled down to wait for night. It was a long wait, and a nervous one.

As darkness approached the wind picked up and the snow started falling harder. Denny looked up into the swirling snowflakes. "Perfect," he said. "Couldn't be better. If we get any kind of head start at all, we'll be safe. Once we get the horses south we'll alter the brands and we're home free with a pocket full of money."

"Sounds good," I said. "But there's still that job next month. Don't you ever take time off?"

"There'll be time enough to enjoy ourselves for a spell," he said. "But I know what you mean. The boss sits warm and cozy back in Deadwood and we do the dirty work. Still, he seems to know where the easy jobs are, and I've made more money in the last year than in the five years before.

"But I'll tell you something. I don't aim to do this much longer. Another six months and I'll have enough money salted away to leave this country and live the way I want."

"How's that?" I asked. "Buy yourself a little ranch in Mexico and stock it with pretty señoritas?"

We were sitting around the fire and Denny's face was plain in the flickering light. He was a smiling, laughing man, but now his voice and expression were both deadly serious.

"I suppose most men would give an arm and a leg to live like that," he said. "But not me.

"You might not know it to look at me, but I'm an easterner. Came out here ten years ago to make my fortune. Never figured to make it dishonest, either, and that's a fact."

"What happened?" I asked. "How'd you get started down this road?"

He sighed and built a smoke. Taking a stick from the fire, he lit the cigarette and inhaled deeply before speaking again. "I had me a girl back east," he said. "Her dad owned a fleet of merchant ships and a house that was big as a hotel. Had servants and all.

"He didn't think I was good enough for his little girl, and let me know it. Guess I can't blame him in some ways. My pa owned a saloon, and ma took in sewing to make ends meet. We were dirt poor, and I never did know what Jennifer saw in me. She was beautiful. Really beautiful. I can close my eyes and still see her black hair and the red of her lips.

"But it was hard on her going against her daddy, so one day I set out to make my fortune, thinking to go back in style and marry her. It didn't work out that way.

"Way I heard it, there was gold all over the west, just waiting to be picked up. But six months after I crossed the Mississippi I was poorer than when I started. The only gold I saw was in a tooth an old prospector had. Then I got a letter from Jennifer.

"During that six months she found herself another man,

one her father approved of. They were going to be married, and she thought I should know.

"Along about that same time a fellow I knew started spending more money than he had a right to. When I asked him about it he clammed up, but one night he got drunk and bragged about rustling some cattle. When he sobered up he told me all about it, and asked if I wanted to ride along next time.

"That was the start of it, and I been riding the owlhoot trail ever since. I've done a lot of things I'm not proud of, and it's time I got out. Figure to head east again when spring comes around. After that, I'm never crossing the Mississippi again, and I'm never taking a dollar that don't belong to me."

Segal spat in the fire. "That's a mighty touching story," he said, "but I like what I'm doing. You won't catch me working for a dollar a day. Not with all the easy pickin's around."

"I don't like having to look over my shoulder all the time to see if the law is closing in," Denny said. "I've been lucky so far, and I've been careful, but sooner or later I know I'm going to look back and see a badge closing in on me.

"Nope. Say what you want, but this is it for me. This job, and the big one next month, and I'm getting out while the getting is good.

"What about you?" Denny asked me. "Young as you are, I guess nothing scares you yet. You ever thought about getting out while there's still time?"

"Haven't given it much thought," I said. "I kind of drifted into the life accidental-like. I'd like to start my own ranch one of these days, but that takes a lot of money."

For a time after that we were all silent, each thinking his own thoughts. Then Denny stood up and kicked snow onto the fire. It sizzled and went out. "The hell with it," he said. "Let's go steal some horses."

CHAPTER 19

THE wind was blowing harder and the snow was falling faster. The weather was still a worry. If it didn't snow enough, tracking the horses would be too easy, but if it snowed too much, driving them anywhere would be difficult or impossible. But that was the life of an outlaw. Speaking for myself, I couldn't see the attraction. Yet I knew how easy it was to drift over the line without really meaning to. I'd heard outlaws talk like Denny before, and many an outlaw wanted nothing more than to get out.

Only most of them stayed over the line too long, rode one midnight trail too many. They got out the hard way . . . by getting in the way of a bullet, or taking a long drop with a short rope around their neck. I was nearly certain that Denny was one of the men who ambushed me and stole Cap, but part of me hoped he would get out and go back east. He was a likable man, one who I thought was basically good.

Yet if the night went as I hoped it would, Denny would soon be in jail, and his dream of going back east might well be dead.

I'd worn a badge more than once in my time, and that was one of the things about it I didn't like. Usually the criminals you arrested had nothing about them to make anyone want to save them. Most often they were hard, callous men who cared nothing for anyone else.

But sometimes they were men who had a wide streak of good in them. Sometimes they were ashamed of the life they led, and wanted out. Thing is, when you wear a badge it isn't your job to decide which is which. A man breaks the law and you arrest him. Then it's up to a judge and jury. There simply wasn't any other way it could work. But I didn't have to like it.

We rode through the cold and snow until we came at last to a spot where there was shelter from the wind. There we pulled up and Denny gave last-minute instructions. "It should take me an' Colorado half an hour, maybe forty-five minutes, to circle around and reach the guard shack," he said. "It shouldn't take more than a few minutes to get the drop on the guards and tie them up. So call it an hour at the outside.

"A little before that, you three ride up to that hilltop there. From this distance you won't be able to see much, but when we have the guards secured I'll wave a lantern in front of the shack. You'll be able to see that without trouble. When you do, move down and start the horses moving. We'll ride down and help as soon as we can.

"Remember. No shooting. If you hear any shots, or you don't see that lantern waving after a reasonable amount of time, it means something went wrong. Turn around and ride back to the last campsite."

"If something does go wrong," Smith asked, "how long do we wait there?"

"Until full light. If we ain't back by then, we probably won't be back at all. Head back to the dugout and warn Blavins, then take the horses there and run. No use taking chances."

Denny turned and rode into the snowstorm without another word and I followed. The cold was forgotten and I focused everything on the job at hand. Waiting until we were nearly a quarter mile from the other men, I eased Strawberry behind Denny. My throat was dry and my heart was beating a little faster than it should have been.

Slipping the thong from my Colt, I eased it out of the holster and thumbed back the hammer. Even in the wind, the sound was harsh and clear. Denny instantly reined his horse to a stop and looked back over his shoulder. It was dark, but I knew he could see the glint of the Colt in my hand.

I heard him sigh. "I half-expected something like this," he said. "Which are you, bounty hunter or the law?"

"There's a badge in my pocket. I'm taking you back to Deadwood."

"On what charge?"

"My name isn't Jim Miller," I said. "It's Jim Darnell. You and another fellow ambushed me a while back. You took my money, my horse, and left me for dead."

For a minute he was silent. "How do you know it was me. Did you see me?"

"Heard your last name is all. You saying it wasn't you?"

"I'm not saying anything. 'Cept you can't prove any of it. Won't do you any good to take me back."

He was probably right. "That might be," I said. "But I'm going to try. Now take your gun out careful and drop it in the snow."

He shoved back his coat and reached for his Colt. "Easy," I said. "You may be fast, but you can't beat a gun in your back at this range."

"Never planned to try," he said. He dropped the gun. Holstering my own Colt, I took the rope from my saddle and shook out a loop and tossed it over Denny. "No need to pin your arms," I said. "Just tighten the loop around your waist."

He did as he was told, and I wrapped my end of the rope around the saddle horn, leaving about fifteen feet of slack between us.

"What about my men?" he asked.

Drawing my Colt again, I pointed it in the air and fired three shots, then quickly reloaded. "If they heard that," I said, "and if they can follow instructions, they should be starting back for the campsite. If not, they'll stay where they are until they realize no lantern is going to show at the guard shack. Either way, they shouldn't be a problem."

"Got it all planned out, haven't you?" Denny asked. "But I wouldn't count on it being that easy."

"I hope it is," I told him. "Anything goes wrong and I might have to shoot you. We'd both hate that."

He said nothing in reply, and I had him turn his horse back the way we came. I hated backtracking our trail, but the lay of the land made it the easiest way to go. Once back a piece, however, I planned to turn north and make sure we came nowhere near the campsite of the previous night.

The snow was still falling and the wind was a cold blast that took away the breath. In the darkness it was impossible to see more than a few yards, and when Denny's men suddenly materialized out of the swirling snow, I don't know who was the more surprised, me or them, but I reacted first.

Had there been time to think I might have reacted in a different way, but there wasn't time to do anything except follow my instincts. Drawing my Colt, I slapped the spurs to Strawberry and yelled at the top of my lungs. Strawberry lunged ahead like he'd been stung by a bee. I slapped Denny's horse on the rump with my Colt as we reached it, then fired twice in the air.

We went right through Denny's men before they could get out of the way. Strawberry slammed into another horse, stumbled, caught his balance. The other horse was walking and unprepared for the sudden contact. It reared onto its hind legs and went over backward. A shot shattered the night, seeming to come from only inches away. Then we were through them and running into the night.

The snow was beginning to pile up and that made running a horse difficult, but trying to stay on high areas where the wind whipped most of the snow away, we made good speed. I didn't know whether or not Denny's men were right behind, or whether they were still trying to recover from the surprise encounter. It was a chance I couldn't take. I pushed on as hard as possible.

After an hour I slowed the horses to an easy walk, but kept

moving. Denny dropped back close enough to talk over the howl of the wind. "That was a damn fool thing to do," he said. "You could have got both of us killed."

"I thought of that," I said. "What were they doing following us, anyway? They should have been making tracks for the campsite."

From the shadow of his face, I saw the glint of teeth and knew he was smiling. "Only a fool trusts a new man completely," he said. "When you were out of earshot I told Toliver to follow us if anything went wrong. Thought I had everything covered. Never figured on you charging right through them."

We kept pushing on until a bit after daylight. The snow had eased, but the wind was still strong and cold. "When are we going to make camp?" Denny asked. "Seems like half my body is frozen solid, not the most unimportant part of which is straddling this saddle."

I knew how he felt. Pushing on through the cold as we'd done was a dangerous thing. I figured the temperature was a bit above zero, but with a wind blowing, frostbite was a serious danger. Looking at our backtrail I saw the wind was covering our tracks almost as quickly as we made them. There was no sign of pursuit.

"Soon as we find a place out of the wind," I said, "we'll make camp. Keep your eyes open."

We both saw the cabin at the same time. It was nearly half a mile away, but built against the side of a hill, it stood dark and clear against the white of the snow. We both turned toward it without a word. After no more than a hundred yards, however, Denny looked back over his shoulder. "There's something wrong," he said. "Look at it. No smoke from the chimney, no sign of life at all."

He was right. The cabin looked deserted. As we drew nearer it became apparent no one lived there. We stopped fifty yards away and looked it over. The door was gone, and one window had no covering. One side of the cabin was scorched . . . as if someone had tried to burn it, but the fire went out before doing too much damage.

"Keep going," I said. "Abandoned or not, it's still shelter."

We pulled up right in front of the cabin and sat looking at it for a minute.

"Slide off your horse and go on in," I said.

Denny did as I told him. Unwrapping the rope from the saddlehorn, I got down and followed him in, keeping the coil of rope in my left hand.

"Walk over to that far wall," I said. "When you get there, very carefully drop any hideouts you have."

He walked to the wall, reached under his coat, and came out with a long-bladed knife. I knew he carried that, but he surprised me when he pulled a derringer from the top of his boot. My Colt was already in my hand and I thumbed the hammer back. "Don't get any ideas," I said. "Lay it on the floor and step away."

He did. "Is that everything?" I asked.

"That's the lot," he said. "Never figured to need that much. You want to search me, go ahead."

"I believe you. Now lay down on the floor and put your hands behind your back."

"Ah, hell," he said. "I was afraid of that. At least tie my hands in front of me. I'll be cramped and sore for a month with 'em tied behind my back."

I nodded. "All right. Flat on your belly. Raise your feet and stretch your hands straight out in front of you."

He lay down, still grumbling. "Hell of a position to put a man in. What's the idea?"

"Only safe way I ever found to tie another man's hands in front of him when you're alone," I said. "If you have any foolish ideas, forget about them. You can't move nearly fast enough lying like that."

"I see what you mean," he said. "You think this up all by yourself?"

"Nope. Had a sheriff show it to me a long time back. Works real well, too."

I hated ruining a good rope, but I sliced off a couple of pieces and tied Denny's hands with one length. With the other piece I tied his ankles, leaving almost two feet of slack between his feet. He could walk like that, but he couldn't run. It's the same way you hobble a horse, and every bit as effective on a man.

That done, I looked about the cabin. It was a large place as cabins go. There were two bedrooms, a large living room, and a kitchen. In the kitchen, next to an uncovered window, I found a skeleton.

There was no sign of clothing on the skeleton, and that made it almost certain the attackers were Indians. So did the way the cabin was ransacked. Indians on the warpath often had to make do without the basics, and the chance to grab warm clothing and anything else of value was always welcome.

Both bedrooms were a mess, but at least I found no other bones. In the smallest bedroom I did find a rocking horse with the head broken off, and other toys scattered about. It sent a shiver through me that had nothing to do with the cold.

Abandoning the search, I set about making the cabin habitable. The front door was lying against a wall, and a quick check showed it was still in good shape despite broken hinges. Standing it back on the door frame, I slid a heavy chair against it to make it stay in place.

There were only two windows to cover, and I made quick work of those with a torn blanket from the bedroom. The work wasn't pretty, but it did the job.

The fireplace was still in good shape, though I worried about the chimney being clogged from disuse. All I could do was build a fire and see what happened. A stack of snow-covered firewood stood near the cabin, but there was enough scattered about the living room to get a fire going. The cabin had been built with knowing hands and it warmed quickly.

That left only food and the horses. We had beans, salt pork, and coffee. The beans would take time to fix, but there was little choice. First, though, I took care of the horses. Dragging the broken bed and a dresser from the bedroom to the living room, I shoved both into a corner. In a few minutes I had the bedroom empty. Then I brought the horses in and let them have the empty room.

In a way I hated doing it. Whoever built the cabin had obviously built it to last, and built it with love. Having horses in the bedroom was the last thing they would have wanted. But the man in the kitchen was beyond caring, and the horses needed warmth and shelter almost as much as we did. They'd been pushed hard, and without rest and heat they might not last the trip to Deadwood.

There was a wood-burning cookstove in the kitchen, and I built a fire there as well. When the stove was hot I melted snow in a large pot and put beans on. It would take three to four hours for them to cook, but some things you can't hurry. I also put on coffee.

Denny had turned a chair back onto its legs and was sitting close to the fire. "Don't know about you," he said, "but I still feel like an icicle."

My feet, hands, and face were all hurting as the heat worked on my skin, but I'd been too wrapped up in doing things to notice. "I know what you mean," I said. "Good thing we found shelter when we did."

Denny held his hands closer to the fire and looked around the room. "I guess so," he said, "but this place bothers me. How long ago you figure all this happened?"

"Hard to tell. Sometime back in the summer, I'd say. The Indian trouble is mostly over this far out of the Black Hills. And it took time and heat to make that skeleton in the kitchen.

"It looks like a woman and a little girl lived here. Wonder what happened to them?"

"You probably don't want to know," Denny said. "Though it may not have been so bad. The Indians might have taken them as prisoners.

"That's hardly an easy life, but it's better than being dead, I guess."

"Maybe."

We stayed in the cabin for three days, waiting for the weather to break. The fourth day dawned bright and sunny and calm. Sometime during the night the temperature had climbed to near the freezing point, and with the sun it felt almost like springtime.

I was glad to be leaving. For three days I'd hustled to find browse for the horses and made innumerable trips outside to the woodpile. And living on beans and salt pork isn't my idea of good food.

I saddled the horses and we started for Deadwood. It felt good to be heading home, and the thought of seeing Mary Kay again made me push Strawberry harder than I might have otherwise.

"You might as well slow down," Denny said. "You're wasting your time taking me in anyway. You can't prove anything, and I'm not about to help you."

"We'll see," I said. "You could make this real easy if you'd just name your boss. It's him I want, not you."

"Can't do it," Denny said. "I never squealed on anybody, and I'm too old to start now."

"Have it your way," I said. "It's your neck."

CHAPTER 20

THE morning we rode into Deadwood a warm wind was blowing and the snow was melting fast. You couldn't really call it a Chinook, but it had pretty much the same effect. It wouldn't last long, I knew, but for the time it did last it felt great.

First thing I did was drop Denny off at the sheriff's office. I explained the story to Sheriff Bullock, and he shook his head. "Be lucky if it even comes to trial," he said. "And we'll never get a conviction."

"I know," I said. "But I figure if we hold him for a time something might break loose. How long do you think you can keep him locked up?"

"Oh, for a while," Bullock said. "I 'spect he'll want a lawyer, but I'll slow things down as much as possible. I doubt I can keep him more than a month. And unless we can dig up some solid evidence, the case'll get laughed right out of court."

That was about what I figured, and all I could do was wait and hope for a lucky break. I handed the badge back to Sheriff Bullock. "Thanks," I said. "I appreciate all your help."

"Just doing my job," he said. "And anytime you want that badge permanent, let me know. I can always use another good man."

I shook my head. "No, I've worn a badge about all I want to. When this trouble is over I want a ranch, and I want to get old and fat and lazy just raising cows and kids."

"Doesn't sound so bad at that . . ." Bullock said.

I said so long and wasted no time getting back to my own

place. Mary Kay saw me coming and met me at the door. Not caring who else was there to see, I scooped her into my arms and kissed her. Carrying her back into the cabin I kicked the door shut behind me and kissed her again.

When I let her up for air her face was flushed. "Welcome home," she said.

"It's good to be back," I said. "Every time I come home from a trip I'm amazed all over again at how beautiful you are."

"I'm glad you think that," she said. "But I hope you never go away again."

"If it was up to me," I said, "I'd never leave you again. Do you think anyone would mind if we locked ourselves in here and never came out?"

Mary Kay laughed. "Owen and Sarah might. They're both in the kitchen right now."

"Story of my life. Well, guess I better put you down and go on in."

Kissing her again, I set her gently on her feet. Mary Kay's eyes are usually green as an emerald, but now and then, when the light is just so, or when she's in a certain mood, they turn a deep gray. Now they were gray . . . and lovely beyond belief. "When's the last time I told you how much I love you?" I asked.

"Too long ago," she said. "Much too long ago."

She put her arms around me and rested her cheek on my chest. "I love you," she said. "More than I can ever tell you."

We walked into the kitchen still holding each other. Owen and Sarah were at the table, and Brennan was bouncing on Owen's knee. "Well, well," Owen said. "The prodigal son returns. How'd it go?"

Taking Brennan and sitting down with him, I told Owen all about it, downplaying the part about Denny's men because of Mary Kay.

"Not much to hold him on," Owen said. "If he keeps his mouth shut he'll likely go free."

"Probably," I said. "But I do have a bit to go on. Denny talked about another job next month, a big one. If I can find out what it is, there's a chance it'll work for us.

"If it's as big as he hinted at, his boss might not want to put it off just because Denny is out of circulation. But that's a long shot.

"Then there's the horse auction down to Cheyenne next month. It's an even longer shot, but I can't help wondering if Cap will be in it. Best way to get rid of a stolen horse I can think of."

"You got that right," Owen said. "The army never was particular about buying stolen horses, so long as nobody raises a fuss. But that's a long, cold ride when there's a better than even chance Cap won't be there."

I nodded. "Figured I'd ask Sheriff Bullock to wire Cheyenne and have someone check it out for me.

"Trouble is, even if Cap is there, it won't prove a thing against Denny. He sold the horses to someone else, and whoever that was may have sold them again. No telling how many people are between the auction and Denny."

"What you need is the boss," Owen said. "But I guess there ain't much reason for Denny to talk. All he has to do is sit tight for a spell and he's free. You have anything else in mind?"

Mary Kay had been busy at the stove, and now she sat a plate of food in front of me. It was piled high with fried potatoes, eggs, and flapjacks. Just the sight of it took my mind off Denny and everything else except eating.

"Yeah," I said. "I plan to eat until I burst. After that I'll worry about Denny."

Pouring molasses over the flapjacks, I dug in and didn't come up for air until the plate was empty. Then I lit a cigar and sipped my coffee. "I wish I could think of something else to try," I told Owen. "But all I can do now is wait for them to make the next move.

"Time's a wastin', and I've given this too much lately. I've got to get busy and earn some money, but it's hard to do that when I have to be looking over my shoulder all the time."

"Might be some good will come out of this after all," Owen said. "When the word gets around that you can't prove anything against Denny they might let up on you."

"How do you mean?"

"Look at it, man. They tried to kill you because they were afraid you could identify Denny and maybe get to whoever the boss is. Now they'll know you can't. Smart thing for them to do will be to leave you alone."

I thought about what he said, and it made sense. But I wasn't sure I liked it. "You might be right," I said. "If I stop digging, they might let it lie. But that gives me an idea.

"What if they think I can identify Denny. What if they think he's willing to make a deal to keep himself out of jail. Think that would stir up the nest?"

"You better believe it," Owen said. "They'd have to kill you then. Or try."

"That's exactly what I thought," I said. "And if we could catch them in the act?"

"Then we really would have something. Catch a man in the act of attempted murder, and he'd be a fool not to talk when it could keep a noose from around his neck."

Mary Kay looked at me like I was crazy. "Of all the dumb ideas you've ever had," she said, "this is the dumbest. What happens if you don't catch them until after they put a bullet in you?"

"It's risky," I said. "No doubt about it. But I can't think of anything else to try."

"Don't worry," Owen said. "Me and the boys will see to it that his back is covered. It just might work, and Jim'll be fine."

Mary Kay shook her head. "Men!" she said. "Sometimes I don't think there's an ounce of brains in the lot of you."

Sarah had been sitting quiet, but now she spoke up. "I've

got to agree with Mary Kay," she said. "And it sure makes me wonder what I'm getting myself into."

Owen blushed and got a sheepish look on his face. "What do you mean?" I asked.

"That's right," Mary Kay said. "You don't know. Owen here swept Sarah right off her feet while you were gone. They're going to be married."

"In two weeks? You convinced her to marry you in two weeks? Guess I underestimated you," I said.

Owen kept his eyes on his coffee cup, but his face was a sight. Sarah slowly shook her head. "I thought somebody needed to take care of the big galoot. Now I'm sure of it. This is the dumbest thing I've ever heard of. You'll both get yourselves killed."

"Aw, honey," Owen said. "You just don't understand. We'll be fine."

"You better be," Sarah said. "I suppose trying to talk you out of this would be wasting my breath."

"It would," Mary Kay said. "Not only are men dumb, they never admit they might be wrong."

Me, I was feeling like a mouse nibbling at bait on a trap. "Owen," I said, "I sure could use a beer about now. How about you?"

He came up from the table and grabbed his coat. "Just what I had in mind," he said. "Let's get!"

I was right behind him. "Aren't you even going to clean up first?" Mark Kay asked. "You're a mess."

"I'll stop in at the barbershop," I said. "Get a bath and a shave. But I wouldn't want Owen to drink alone."

She started to say something else, but we were out the door and gone. Once into Deadwood we saw Thomas and Henry Walsh coming out of the mercantile. We waved them over, and they walked to the saloon with us. The beer was cold and went down smooth. While we drank we talked about Estle Denny.

Thomas and Henry both allowed the plan we had might

work and agreed to help in any way they could. "Raymond will want in," Thomas said. "You can count on it. Between the four of us, protecting your back should be a cinch."

"We'd best talk it over with the sheriff," Henry said. "Denny is his prisoner. Seems to me he should know what we're up to."

"Hadn't thought of that," I said, "but you're right. I'll talk to him this evening."

"Talk to him right now, if you want," Owen said. "Yonder he comes."

Looking back over my shoulder, I saw Sheriff Bullock heading our way. He walked up to the table and clapped a hand down on my shoulder. "Didn't think you'd leave your cabin for a week," he said. "What happened, did your wife run you off?"

"Something like that," I said. "Sit down and I'll tell you all about it."

He sat down and I laid the plan out for him. When I finished he took off his hat and scratched his head. "It might work," he said. "But you're sure painting a target on your back. How you going to get the word around?"

"No problem," Owen said. "Just follow my lead."

Owen raised his voice so half the saloon could hear what he said. "It's about time we cleared out the murderers," he said. "Now watch them run. Why, thanks to Jim here, we got them dead to rights."

A man at a nearby table took the bait. "What are you talking about?" he asked. "What murderers?"

"The ones who've been killing all the miners and blaming it on Indians," Owen said loudly. "But Jim brought the one in who ambushed him. Saw him plain when it happened, and now he's in jail."

"He named any names?" a man asked.

"Not yet," Owen said. "But you can bet he will. With Jim as a witness, Denny is facing a noose, and well he knows it. He'll talk before he'll hang. You can bet on that."

It was all I could do to keep from grinning. "Did you really see him shoot at you?" the man asked.

"Saw him plain, just like Owen said. But it's his boss I want. Sheriff Bullock here agrees with me. We figure if we let Denny walk, he'll name his boss sure."

"You really think he'll talk?"

"Wouldn't you?" I asked. "Sure beats hanging."

I could see men all around the saloon talking about what we'd said, and I knew it would be all over Deadwood in a matter of hours. "Well," I said. "That's that. Wonder when the shooting will start?"

"I don't know," Bullock said. "But I can see the target on you now. Let's walk back to my office. We've got some plans to make."

CHAPTER 21

IN the sheriff's office we sat down and outlined the best way to protect me while still giving someone the chance to put a bullet in my back. Then, against their protests, I made Mary Kay, Sarah, and Brennan move into the Grand Hotel.

That taken care of, the waiting began. For three full days I moved around as usual, but every second there were at least two rifles covering me. Sometimes it was Owen and Henry, sometimes Sheriff Bullock and Thomas, but whoever it was, they stayed out of sight. I knew where they were, of course, and never strayed from protected areas.

But it was still a risky business, and well I knew it. Someone might get off a shot before we could stop him. So for three days I walked around with the hair on the back of my neck standing straight up. It wasn't a pleasant feeling.

Then, about four in the morning of the third night, they made their move—only trouble was, they didn't make it on me.

Estle Denny was in jail, and he had round-the-clock protection. Even the window to his cell was covered with a shutter. Between that and iron bars, plus a deputy always on duty, we thought he would be safe. Only someone thought he made an easier target than I did. They were nearly right.

His window opened to an alley, and in the night the killer propped a ladder against the wall to reach his window, carefully pried the shutter open, stuck a pistol between the bars and blasted away. Fortunately, the cell was poorly lit and Denny heard the shutter being pried open. He sat up on his cot, still groggy from sleep, and looked around. When the pistol came through the bars he rolled onto the floor. But there wasn't much in the way of cover and even moving as he was, two bullets found their mark.

Both wounds were little more than burns, one across the ribs and a second along the side of his neck. They didn't even bleed much. But they made Denny mad as hell.

Sheriff Bullock was sleeping then, and Owen and Henry were watching the cabin while I slept. The deputy woke the sheriff, and he came to wake me. When I reached the jail, Owen and Henry close behind, the doctor was just finishing his work on Denny.

Denny was swearing to beat the band, when he looked around and saw me. "They tried to kill me," he said. "I wasn't about to talk, but they tried to kill me. You still want to know who my boss is?"

"I do, if you're the one who ambushed me," I said.

Putting his hand to the bandage on his neck, Denny touched it gingerly and looked at the floor. Then he asked if there was any hot coffee. The deputy brought him a cup after the sheriff nodded.

"I'm the one," Denny said. "Me and Solomon Smith. You may not believe this, but that's the first time I ever shot at anyone who wasn't looking me in the eye. And I felt awful about it afterward.

"Fact is, right after that was when I decided to pull out for good. I might be a lot of things, but a backshooter ain't one of them. I hope you believe that."

"I believe it," I said.

"Good. Now, as for the boss. His name is Collin Driscoll. Don't know if you've heard of him, but he's behind half the murders and thefts around here.

"Next month he plans to hit a gold shipment going out from the McAleer and Pierce claim. There's supposed to be better than a hundred thousand in gold, if Driscoll knows what he's talking about. And he always does."

"He does this time," Sheriff Bullock said. "Most of the miners keep me informed about shipments like that, and one hundred thousand is right on the nose. But there'll be half a dozen armed guards along with the shipment. And that's not counting the driver and regular shotgun rider. Nobody in his right mind would try taking that one. Too many easier scores around."

"That's true enough," Denny said, "but Driscoll is planning to take it just the same. Two of the guards are his men. When the others ride out to hold up the coach, those two will get the drop on the guards."

"Which guards work for Driscoll?" Sheriff Bullock asked.

"I don't know," Denny said. "And that's the gospel."

"No matter," Sheriff Bullock said. "If you're willing to say all this again in court, Driscoll will be behind bars as soon as I get a warrant for him. And that will be first thing tomorrow morning."

We talked a spell longer, then called it a night. But not before Sheriff Bullock asked the lot of us to meet him at the jail before nine in the morning. "I can use more deputies than I have," he said. "Besides, I figure you all deserve to be in on this."

"Thanks," I said. "I'm looking forward to it."

That's the way we left it, and I walked back to the cabin. Owen and Henry came with me, but this time we all went inside and had more coffee. Driscoll had made his try at Denny, and it was unlikely he would send someone after me now.

After a bit we tried to get some sleep, but I doubt any of us got more than two hours. Yet we were all awake and alert by seven. We went back down into Deadwood and had breakfast at the Grand Central with Mary Kay and Sarah before going to the jail.

When we got to the jail the sheriff was gone, and one of his deputies said he was down trying to get his warrant.

Sheriff Bullock came in a half hour later, and he was mad. Before explaining anything he told his two deputies to get down to the Badlands and stand watch on the Saratoga Saloon.

"Driscoll has a room there," he said, "and does most of his gambling there. Go inside just as if it's a regular check. If you see Driscoll, don't pay any attention to him. Get back outside and watch the place. Nothing else."

The deputies went out and Sheriff Bullock dropped into a chair. I gave him a cup of coffee and he sipped it. He stroked his mustache and explained the trouble. "I went to Judge McClean and asked for a warrant," Bullock said. "Fine, the judge tells me, only I'm busy now. Tell me who it's on and come back around noon."

Thomas looked puzzled. "What's wrong with that?" he asked. "It only means we'll have to wait a couple more hours."

"That's almost three hours from now," I said. "Might be the word will get out, and if it does, Driscoll will run."

"You think the judge is crooked?"

"Probably not," Bullock said. "But he is an idiot, and he's got a loose mouth. He asked me who the warrant was for with a dozen people listening. I tried to get him in private, but he wouldn't budge.

"No, he's likely honest, but that doesn't help. I can almost guarantee word will reach Driscoll. Hell, he might know already. If he doesn't run it'll be a miracle."

"He'll run," I said. "The moment he knows about the warrant, he'll run. He might already be on his way."

Raymond Walsh came through the door then, and he was shaking snow off his clothing. "Looks like a bad storm brewing," he said. "If it don't turn into a full-blown blizzard I'll be surprised. Temperature's dropping, too."

"Maybe that will keep Driscoll here even if he does get word," Henry said. "We've been lucky this winter, but we're overdue for another bad spell."

I poured a cup of coffee and dropped into a chair. Sipping it slowly, I thought about Driscoll. Trouble was, I didn't know enough about him. There was simply no way to tell how he would react to learning he was going to be arrested. He might stay and try to beat the charge in court, he might fight, or he might run.

After a time I got up and poured another cup of coffee, then filled a second cup and carried it back to the holding area where Estle Denny's cell was. He took the cup of coffee through the bars.

"Something I been meaning to ask you," I said. "It's about my horse. Cap and I have been through a lot together."

"I 'spect so," Denny said. "Never seen a finer animal. Don't worry, he's all right."

I let out a breath I didn't know I'd been holding. "I'm glad to hear that. I was afraid you'd shot him."

"I thought about it," he said. "When I heard you were still alive, I surely thought about it. Shooting him would have been the smart thing to do, and no doubt about it. But I've had a good horse a time or two myself."

"Where is he then? Did you take him down for that army auction in Cheyenne?"

"Not a chance. You ever see how they treat horses? Nope, I gave him to a friend for safekeeping. Right after that job next month I was going to pull out, head east, and I was going to do it on your horse."

We talked a piece, and Denny told me where Cap was and gave me directions on how to get there. He also wrote me out a note telling his friend to let me have the horse. "Nate doesn't know he's stolen," Denny said. "And he's a man who likes horses, so he's taken good care of him. I saw to that."

"I appreciate that," I said. "I ought to want you hanging from a tall tree for ambushing me. But you been stand-up straight with us, and you took care of Cap. I'll talk to Sheriff Bullock. Far as I'm concerned there's nothing to charge you with."

Denny looked at me over his coffee. "You mean that? You wouldn't press charges against me for shooting you?"

"I'm probably a damn fool," I said. "But no, you testify

against Driscoll if it comes to court, and I'll forget I ever heard of you."

Denny stood up and extended his hand. "You don't have to shake it," he said, "but it would be a pleasure."

I shook his hand. After a few minutes I went back into the office and told Sheriff Bullock what I'd decided about Denny. "It's your choice," he said. "No telling how many rustlings and the like he's been connected with over the years, but there's not a one I can charge him with. He isn't wanted for anything. If you won't press charges against him, he's a free man. But I think you're making a mistake."

"It wouldn't be the first one," I said, "and probably not the last. But I think Denny is a good man. He's ridden outside the law a good part of his life, but I think he means it when he says he's going straight.

"Anyway, that's how I want to play it. When this is over, he can ride out. Agreed?"

Bullock shrugged. "Like I said, he isn't wanted for a thing. You don't press charges and he's a free man."

We sat around and drank coffee until noon, then Sheriff Bullock walked back to the courthouse. He came back a short time later with the warrant. He handed out badges all around.

"Time to get this over with," he said. "Let's go find Driscoll."

We slipped into our coats, checked our guns, and walked out of the jail and down the street. Our faces were hard, our thoughts locked on what lay ahead. There were five of us, plus the two deputies already watching the Saratoga. There was no way of knowing how many men Driscoll might have, or if they would put up a fight.

I wasn't feeling particularly brave about it, and I didn't think the other men were, either. It was simply a thing that had to be done, and it was up to us to do it.

CHAPTER 22

WE checked with the deputies and found they hadn't seen a sign of Driscoll, inside or out. "Well," Sheriff Bullock said, "we won't find him standing out here in the cold. Let's go see if Mr. Driscoll is home."

Four of us went in through the front, three through the back. The Saratoga was crowded, and it was my guess that any of the men there had reason to fear the law. One stood up quickly and tried to draw his gun as we came in, but Sheriff Bullock chopped him on the side of the neck with the barrel of his Colt and the man went down.

While the rest of us kept an eye on the crowd, Sheriff Bullock walked to be bar and looked the bartender in the eye.

"Which room is Driscoll's?" he asked.

"Never heard of him," the bartender said.

Sheriff Bullock reached across the bar and caught the bartender by his shirt. With one good pull he jerked the bartender half across the bar. His grip was high on the man's shirt, closing it tight around the neck. It didn't take long for the bartender's face to turn beet red from lack of air. Sheriff Bullock looked at him nose to nose. "If your memory doesn't improve," he said, "I'm going to drag you all the way to the jail like this. Which room?"

The bartender had a time trying to talk, but he managed to gasp that Driscoll's room was at the top of the stairs and all the way down the hall. Sheriff Bullock shoved the bartender hard enough to slam him against the wall behind the bar. Half a dozen whiskey bottles bounced and fell, shattering when they hit the floor.

Bullock looked up the stairs. "Let's get it done," he said.

The bartender was rubbing his neck. "Won't do you any good," he said. "Mr. Driscoll ain't up there."

"Where is he?" Bullock asked.

"I—I don't know," the bartender said. "He took a bunch of the boys and left, a couple of hours back. Went out in a real hurry."

"And you don't know where he went?"

The bartender shook his head. We went up the stairs and checked the room anyway, but Driscoll was gone. The room was a mess. Clothes were strewn about, and all the drawers in the bureau were open.

"Looks like he was in a hurry," Thomas said. "Took what he could carry and left."

"We'd best check the liveries," Sheriff Bullock said. "But I'm willing to bet he's already out of Deadwood."

He was. Forty-five minutes later we found the livery where he'd kept his horse. The owner wasn't around, but a boy of about fifteen was there. "They rode out to the east," he told us. "Seemed in an awful hurry."

"How many men did he have with him?" I asked.

"Six, I think. Maybe two more outside. At least I think those two were with him."

The snow was coming down so thick it was hard to see across the street. "If the wind picks up," Sheriff Bullock said, "this will turn into a first-class blizzard. A man would have to be a fool to go riding off in this weather."

"Guess Driscoll figured it would be better than jail," I said. "What now?"

"Now we go after him. If we hurry, we might find his trail before it's snowed over."

"I thought you didn't have jurisdiction outside of Deadwood?"

"You thought right. But I don't want Driscoll getting away. Likely we're too late, but I mean to try."

We tried. Quickly putting together a bit of food and other

supplies, we rode out, hoping to pick up the trail. Sheriff Bullock knew his business, and Owen proved a good tracker as well. We found the trail, lost it in the blowing snow, found it again.

But with the wind picking up and the snow falling harder than ever, it was a losing battle. Darkness came and the temperature dropped out of sight. "We've got to hunt shelter for the night," Sheriff Bullock said. "If we don't, we'll freeze."

"By morning there won't be a trace of them left," I said. "Looks like they've made it."

"Maybe," Thomas said, "and maybe not. They won't be able to ride in this either. They'll have to find shelter and wait out the storm just like us. We might still have a chance."

"Not much of one," Owen said. "Driscoll is three hours or more ahead of us. I don't think we'll ever see him again."

We made camp and waited out the storm. When morning came it eased off a good bit, but there was two feet of fresh snow on the ground. We spent the day riding wide circles, trying to cut his sign. We found nothing. We spent one more night in the cold, then reluctantly turned back to Deadwood.

I had mixed feelings about the whole thing. Driscoll was gone, and so, I hoped, was the danger. That was something, but it nagged at me that he'd gotten away. He'd paid to have me shot and my money stolen, and he was responsible for who knew how many murders and holdups. The thought of him going somewhere else and starting it all over again rankled.

But if nothing else, it meant I was free to get back to the business at hand. I still needed money in the worst way, and time was running out.

One of the first things we did after getting back to Deadwood was to let Estle Denny out of jail. With Driscoll gone there was little point in holding him, but Sheriff Bullock did ask him to stay around town for a few weeks just in case Driscoll turned up again.

He asked the sheriff for permission to leave Deadwood for

a few days, promising to return before the week was out. Bullock didn't like it, but told him to go ahead.

Denny rode out and came back exactly a week later. When he returned he brought Cap with him. Me, I'd been planning to ride out and get Cap myself, but knew it would be a time before I could get away. Denny brought him up to my cabin, and it was like seeing an old friend again.

I asked Denny if he wanted to come in for coffee, and he looked down at the ground for a minute, then back at me.

"I'd like to," he said. "Don't know about meeting your wife, though. How will she take to me being here . . . after me putting that bullet in you and all."

"Don't worry about that," I said. "She's a fine woman."

He nodded and stepped down off his horse. "Let me get Cap put away," I said, "and we'll go in."

Taking Cap down to the stable I'd built, I rubbed him down and gave him enough grain to fill his belly. "He's fat and sassy," I told Denny. "You took good care of him."

"Like I said, I've never seen a better horse. Besides, a man in my line of work best take care of his horse. It can mean your life if he gets winded at the wrong time."

We went into the cabin and I introduced Denny to Mary Kay. She extended her hand and he took it. "I'm very pleased to meet you," Mary Kay said. "But I hope you find another way to earn a living from now on."

Denny had his hat in his hand, and he blushed a little. "Yes, ma'am," he said.

"You're welcome here. Anytime you like. Now, we have hot coffee, but it's nearly lunchtime. Won't you eat with us?"

"Yes, ma'am. I'd be honored."

We sat down at the kitchen table with a cup of hot coffee while Mary Kay worked up a quick lunch. When she left the room for a minute to get Brennan, Denny looked at me. "You told it true," he said. "She is a special lady. You're a lucky man, Darnell."

"I know it," I said.

Mary Kay came back into the kitchen holding Brennan. She started to hand him to me, but Denny asked if he could hold him. "If he'll let you," she said. "Sometimes he's shy around strangers."

Estle Denny put out his hands and Brennan fell right into them. He stood on Denny's lap and laughed. "Never was around kids much," Denny said, "but I always thought I'd like to have a boy of my own."

"It's not too late," Mary Kay said. "You're still young. Have you thought about getting married and settling down?"

"Ma'am," he said. "I've thought about it, but with the life I've been leading, well, it just wasn't possible."

"My husband tells me you're going back east. It shouldn't be difficult to find a good woman there."

"Figure to pull out as soon as the sheriff says he doesn't need me anymore. I'd like to start fresh where nobody knows me. That reminds me, I've something for the two of you."

He'd taken off his coat when he came into the cabin, and it was hanging on a hook near the door. He stood up and walked to the coat, took an envelope from the pocket, and came back to the table. He tossed the envelope to me. It was full of money.

"There's fifteen thousand dollars there," he said. "Fact is, I only got to keep five thousand of your money an' Driscoll took the rest, but I wouldn't feel right unless I gave it all back. I know it doesn't make up for what I did, but it's a start."

"I'll take it," I said, "and thanks. But won't this leave you short for heading back east?"

He smiled. "That job next month would have put me over the top," he said, "but I'm a long way from being broke, even after giving you that."

Mary Kay put out the food and we dug in, Brennan doing his share to keep up.

After lunch I lit a cigar and gave one to Denny. He lit it

and leaned back in his chair. Mary Kay told me she was going down to see Sarah.

"Where is Sarah?" I asked.

"Working at the mercantile today. I have to take some sewing back to a man, so I'll stop and see her on the way. I'll take Brennan with me."

She bundled Brennan up and slipped into her coat. When she was gone we drank more coffee. Denny helped me clear the table. "One thing I did want to see you alone about," he said. "I'm not so sure Driscoll has left the area."

My heart jumped a little. "What makes you say that?"

"Partly a feeling, partly because I know him. I wasn't the only man he had working for him. Not by a long shot.

"I never did a killing for him, but he was sure behind a bunch. Me, I stole horses and cattle, sometimes stuck up a stage or a gold shipment, but I always planned ahead and made sure there was no shooting.

"Driscoll wasn't so careful. I backed out on half a dozen jobs because I thought they were too risky, but he'd always find someone to do them. I think he's still going to try for that gold shipment."

"Sheriff Bullock will replace his men," I said. "He'll have to go against eight guns. Is he that big a fool?"

"He left Deadwood with maybe eight men, and my boys will join him if he's still around. If that's not enough he can find more. He'll find a good spot and ride out with a dozen or more men."

"How sure of this are you?"

"Call it fifty-fifty," he said. "It just isn't like him to let a thing go, is all."

"I think you may be right. Let's go down and talk to the sheriff."

"Think he'll believe me?"

"Yeah, I think he will. Might be we're wrong, but if we're right, this could be our chance. If we play it right, we might still nail Driscoll."

CHAPTER 23

IT took some fast talking to convince the sheriff, but at last he gave in. "I guess it won't hurt anything to look at it your way," he said. "If we're wrong, it's no more than wasted time. If we're right, we have a chance to stop Driscoll once and for all."

"Did you find out which guards belonged to Driscoll?"

"As a matter of fact, I did. Can't prove a thing, but two of the men have warrants on them out of Texas. Can't arrest them here unless they commit a crime, but they're the ones."

"You fired them yet?" Denny asked.

"No, I haven't," Sheriff Bullock said. "I just learned about the warrants yesterday. Figured to go down to McAleer and Pierce's sometime this evening."

"Don't do it," Denny said. "Let them keep their jobs."

"What! Are you crazy? I can't let them ride guard on that gold shipment. Driscoll would—wait a minute, I think I see what you're getting at."

"So do I," I said. "If those men aren't fired Driscoll is bound to think we weren't told about him planning to steal the gold. He'll think he still has men on the inside and he might not come in shooting."

"That's the way I'd play it," Denny said. "And no bragging intended, but I think I know a little more about that side of the business than you two."

Sheriff Bullock tapped a match against his desk. "How do we go about it?" he asked. "We still can't let those two ride guard."

"Let them ride out of Deadwood with the gold," Denny said. "Have a couple of men waiting along the trail to replace

158

them, and a deputy to bring them back. Put the new men in their coats and hats, and Driscoll won't know until it's too late what he's riding into."

"No wonder you never got caught," Sheriff Bullock said. "What do you think, Darnell?"

"I think we're going to catch Driscoll in the act," I said. "And I want to be there when it happens. I'd like to replace one of those men myself.

"Something else, though. We're still going to be outnumbered. Might not be a bad idea to get a dozen or so men together and have them follow the gold shipment at a safe distance."

"Good idea," Sheriff Bullock said. "Do you think Owen and the others will want in on it?"

"I don't even have to ask them," I said. "They'll want in on it, all right."

Denny adjusted his hat. "Neither of you has a reason to trust me," he said, "but I want in on this too."

"I'll tell you the truth," Sheriff Bullock said. "I'm not sure I do trust you. This conversion of yours has been a little quick, don't you think?"

"My conversion has nothing to do with it," Denny said. "I worked for Driscoll, and he tried to have me killed. I want a chance to even things up a bit. Whatever I've done, I never once turned on a friend. Driscoll has something coming, and I want to be there when he gets it."

"Now that I can believe," Sheriff Bullock said. "What do you think, Darnell?"

"I think he deserves a chance," I said. "Put him with me and we'll replace Driscoll's guards. Be worth it just to see Driscoll's face when he sticks up the gold shipment and sees our faces under the hats his men were wearing."

Sheriff Bullock smiled. "I'd like to see that myself," he said. "All right, Denny, as of now you're in. But I still have my doubts, so humor me and stay close."

"Whatever it takes," Denny said. "For a shot at Driscoll I'd sit in one of your cells until it's time to ride out."

That's the way we left it, but there was still a ton of details to iron out. Sheriff Bullock worked on those while I began going about the business of finding myself a ranch. It was still a bit over two weeks before the gold shipment was leaving, and I'd lost enough time already. Again, Estle Denny was a big help.

He knew nearly every rancher in the territory, had stolen horses or cattle from many of them, in fact, but luckily for him they didn't know that. He rode out with me to see a rancher named Erskine Marlowe who was wanting to sell out. Marlowe was a youngish man, tall, redheaded, and pleasant.

He took us on a snowbound tour of his holdings, and the high points took the better part of a day and a half.

"I wish you could see her at high summer," he said. "She's as pretty a ranch as you'll ever find. Good land, good grass, plenty of water. Got everything a rancher could wish."

It did look good. Even under almost three feet of snow, it looked good. Almost too good. "I can't see much to find fault with," I said, "but if it's all you claim, why sell it?"

"I'm not a rancher and don't pretend to be. My father bought this ranch and had a fool notion of us spending the rest of our lives here.

"Well, he spent the rest of his here. He's buried not far from the ranch house. I'm going back to civilization before the same thing happens to me."

Casting a glance at Denny I saw him wink at me. "How much do you want for it?" he asked. "Land, cattle, buildings, everything."

Marlowe rubbed his chin. "Well, there's a fine breeding herd here. Near four hundred head of young stuff and just enough bulls to go around. Figure them at ten thousand dollars.

"Then you have the land itself. I own title to four thousand acres, and that's going for a good bit. Let's say twenty thousand as she stands."

"Let's go, Denny," I said. "It's going to be a long ride back to Deadwood."

"Wait a minute," Marlowe said. "I thought you were interested in buying the place?"

"Not at those prices," I said. "Somebody's been pulling your leg about the value of things. Granted, if you round up all those cattle and drove them to market, you might get your asking price. But they aren't rounded up, and from the looks of it, they never will be. If you don't drift them into shelter and feed them a lot of hay they won't last till spring.

"As for the land, only a bit of what you own is really valuable, and that's the bit with running water on it. The rest is good grazing land, but folks are near giving that away."

"How am I supposed to get all those cattle together and feed them?" he asked. "They'll find plenty of grass under the snow, won't they?"

"A few might," I said. "But this winter is barely under way. Most of them won't make it without help. No, I guess we better ride."

"Now hold on! What will you offer for the ranch?"

"I'll give you five thousand," I said. "Hard cash. That's enough to set yourself up well in a city."

"That's not much for all this," he said. "Can't you make it ten thousand?"

"No. I'll go a thousand dollars higher, and that's it. And that offer is good for today only. You ride into Deadwood with us and we do the paperwork this evening. A stage leaves Deadwood in two days, and it'll take you wherever you want to go."

For a minute he sat there looking first at me, then at Denny. "All right," he said at last. "Six thousand it is. Let's get it over with."

We rode back to Deadwood and went straight to the bank. A few minutes after that I owned a ranch. I told Marlowe to take whatever personal belongings he wished when he left, and he told me his clothes were all he wanted.

From the bank he went to a hotel and checked in. I walked with Denny back to my cabin. Along the way I got to wondering why Denny couldn't look at me without grinning.

"What's the matter with you?" I asked. "You think I cheated him?"

"No, I think he cheated himself. What I don't understand is how you knew his cattle were scattered to hell and gone? We only saw a few head, and they looked pretty well fed. For all I knew he had every head he owned tucked in a draw and loaded down with hay. How'd you know?"

"I didn't. Just took a chance, was all. Those cattle we saw were in areas out of the wind. They'd found a spot where the grass was tall enough and thick enough to get at, and where nothing could get at them without trouble."

"So what?"

"Hell, man. You've stolen enough cattle to know they generally stay together in the winter, or they scatter all over the place. Those fat yearlings just looked wrong. Thing is, they looked too perfect."

"You think he put them there for you to see?"

"That was the way I read it. He wanted me, or whatever buyer came along, to think his herd was in good shape. But he missed one thing."

"What's that?"

"What's the most valuable animal on a ranch?"

"A good breeding bull. Why?"

"You see any bulls with those yearlings?"

"Damn. Now that you mention it, there wasn't one."

"Yet he claimed to have several. If he had any idea where they were he'd have taken us to them. That alone could have jumped his asking price. Least that's what I figured after a time."

"Damndest thing I ever saw. You figured all that out just because you didn't see a bull?"

"Not really. Just took a chance. Marlowe wasn't a rancher, and showed it. Man has to love ranching to keep a herd together and fed in this weather."

Denny was still shaking his head when we walked into the cabin. The place was empty, but there was a note from Mary Kay saying she'd be back before dark.

As I was reading the note she came through the door. She asked what I'd been up to, and Estle said I'd been giving him lessons in stealing cattle. Mary Kay looked puzzled and he laughed. "I don't mean that seriously," he said. "But if he can round them up, and that's iffy in this weather, your husband just made himself a killing."

I explained about the ranch and Mary Kay smiled. "Sounds like you made a fair deal, all things considered," she said. "But I do feel sorry for his father. He must have wanted a ranch pretty bad."

"Don't let that worry you none," Denny said. "I knew his father. He was a good man, but he didn't know much more about ranching than his son. That ranch would have gone under this winter even if the old man was still alive."

"Perhaps it would have," Mary Kay said, "but I still feel for him."

"So do I, in a way," I said. "On the other hand, you could say he got what he wanted."

"You'll have to explain that," she said.

"He may not have known anything about ranching, but I do. That's good land, and I'll round up the herd, or enough of it to build a fine place. That ranch will be a beauty, Mary Kay, and he's buried there.

"I hope when my time comes I'll be as lucky. A man could do worse than be buried on a piece of land where the cattle roam free and people who care look after things."

"I can't argue with that," she said. "So we're back in the ranching business?"

"That we are," I said. "That we are."

CHAPTER 24

DEADWOOD was full of men who couldn't find any work at all, and it wasn't hard to find a couple who knew a bit about cattle. With their help, and Denny's, I spent most of every day rounding up cattle. The ranch was so close to Deadwood that the ride was an easy one, and I couldn't have asked for better.

We made progress, but the day came when my attention had to turn back to the gold shipment. The evening before it was to leave, Sheriff Bullock brought us all together and made sure we all knew what was going on. About the only change he made that Driscoll might notice was replacing the shotgun guard. Sheriff Bullock would do that himself.

"That's a common enough thing on a shipment of this size," he said. "Driscoll will notice, but it shouldn't spook him any."

"It won't," Denny said. "He'll almost expect that."

"Good," Sheriff Bullock said. "It's settled then. Darnell, you and Denny will meet us on the trail outside of Deadwood. You'll replace Driscoll's guards, and my deputy will bring them back to the jail.

"Owen, you and the other men will follow along about a mile back. You probably won't get there before the shooting stops unless they get the better of us. That shouldn't happen, but if it does, you come in firing.

"Even if everything goes right, a couple of them will likely slip away, and you boys can round them up. Are we all clear?"

We were. It would all start before dawn, but I knew the night would still be a long one. Denny stayed in my cabin that night, and we were both up and at the breakfast table three hours before first light.

I told Mary Kay she could stay in bed and get more sleep, but she wouldn't hear of it. "I won't sleep a wink until you get back," she said. "I may as well see you off with a good breakfast in your belly."

Still in the quiet darkness of our bedroom, with her warmth all around me, and with our baby breathing softly in his own small bed, I took her in my arms. "I fell in love with you the moment I first looked into those beautiful green eyes of yours," I said. "But as much as I loved you then, I love you even more now."

She snuggled closer and I felt the warmth of her breast press against me. "Then make me a promise," she said. "For me, for Brennan, promise me this will be the last bloodshed. Promise me that when this is over you'll put away your guns."

For a time I said nothing, but I knew how much it meant to her. "I've never made you a promise I didn't think I could keep," I said. "But I will promise one thing. This country is growing fast. Hundreds and thousands of people are coming in by the month. Before long there won't be a need for every man to wear a gun.

"I promise you this, Mary Kay . . . the very instant I think I can hang up my guns without putting you and Brennan in danger, I'll do it."

"I guess that's all I can really ask," she said. "Except for one thing."

"What's that?"

"Kiss me. Kiss me and love me like you'll never leave my side."

She turned her face up to mine and I kissed her. If her eyes were beautiful, her lips were like wild honey. Kissing them was as much as my life was worth.

Yet time passed and all too soon I had to leave the bed. It didn't put me in the best of moods, though it helped that she arose with me and cooked breakfast. One of the things I've always loved about Mary Kay is her intelligence and her ability to do just about anything a man can do, and do it better. But I'll tell you, few things are more pleasant than having a woman prepare a meal.

After breakfast it was time for me and Denny to put on our coats and step out into the cold. I didn't want to go. Down that cold trail I could catch a bullet and die.

It wasn't that being killed scared me. But losing Mary Kay did, and that's what a bullet would mean. It made me irritable. In fact, it made me mad as hell. All I wanted to do was stay in the warmth of the cabin with the woman I loved. But because of one man's greed I had to leave that warmth.

If Collin Driscoll crossed my path down that cold trail, I was going to make him pay for every bit of it.

We'd arranged to meet one of Sheriff Bullock's deputies along the trail outside of Deadwood, and we found him easily enough.

The temperature couldn't have been much above zero, and a cold north wind made it seem much worse. Thing that bothered me most, however, was the waiting. We'd ridden out before dawn to avoid being seen, but the gold shipment wasn't due along for several hours. And there was no way we could sit out in the open for that long without suffering frostbite.

"Let's find a place overlooking the trail," I said. "Out of the wind. I don't know about you two, but I could use a cup of hot coffee about now."

"Amen," the deputy said. "I know just the spot, too."

He led us to a spot about a quarter mile down the trail, and about two hundred yards off to the side. The land swelled up and offered a natural windbreak, while wood was easily found in the form of dead limbs still clinging to trees.

All three of us carried tin cups and coffee, and the deputy had thought to bring a pot. With a small fire going, we melted snow and made coffee. The pot held just enough to give us each a cup with a bit left over. I'd a hunch we'd make several pots before the gold shipment came along.

It was still too cold to be comfortable, but with the small fire and the hot coffee, we made due. To pass the time and keep our minds off the cold, we talked. The deputy's name was Will Clark, and he was Indiana born and Illinois bred. He was young, only twenty, and had been west less than a year.

We drank coffee and swapped stories until a bit after nine. Then Denny looked down the trail, swallowed the last of his coffee, and stood up. He began kicking snow on the fire. "What are you doing that for?" Clark asked. "I was about to make more coffee."

"No time," Denny said. "Look down the trail there."

We looked. The wagon and the guards were in sight, looking dark and large against the snow. "We'd best mount up," I said. "Looks like the fun is over."

We rode down slowly to meet the gold shipment. Sheriff Bullock was sitting next to the driver and riding shotgun. The guards on horseback rode two before, two behind, and two flanking. Turned out Sheriff Bullock had Driscoll's two men riding ahead.

They looked almighty puzzled when every man around them pointed a gun in their direction, but even armed with double-barreled shotguns, they weren't about to make a fight of it.

We disarmed them and switched hats and coats with them. One of the men wore black boots with bright silver inlay on them, and since I'd taken his hat and coat, I also took the boots. There was always a chance Driscoll would notice if I didn't, so in spite of the fact that they were at least a size too small, I slipped into them.

Will Clark took the two back toward Deadwood, and we started on down the trail. Denny and I both kept the borrowed coats pulled up around our faces and the brims of the hats pulled low. From any distance at all he'd be certain we were his men.

The only change we made was riding behind the wagon instead of in front of it. "Those two wanted to ride back there in the worst way," Sheriff Bullock said. "I figure that's where Driscoll wanted them."

"Makes good sense," I said. "From back there his two men could have cut you apart had anything started."

So that's where we rode, our hands always close to the trigger and our eyes searching every bit of cover. The one thing we wanted to make Driscoll do was get close. If he had an ambush set up where his men could open up from cover all our plans would be for nothing.

With that in mind we rode well away from any possible ambush spots, even if it meant fighting drifts. We had to force Driscoll into the open, and that was the only way.

Yet the first day passed with nothing at all happening. So did the second day. Halfway through the third day I was beginning to wonder if Driscoll had decided the job was too dangerous and was going to pass.

Then, along about three in the afternoon of the third day, we saw a group of riders coming down the trail, riding bold as you please. From any distance at all they looked like just another bunch of would-be miners heading for Deadwood.

Thing is, had his two men still been riding behind the wagon, it would have been a fine plan. With two shotguns behind, and all his men in front, it would have been easy pickings. Only we'd changed all that. When they were no more than twenty yards ahead, Denny and me both spurred our horses and rode out front where the action was to be.

Driscoll was riding behind the group, not wanting to be recognized, but our riding up front like that threw everything out of kilter. Driscoll's men pulled up and looked confused, and in the confusion Driscoll had to push toward the front to see what had gone wrong.

By that time we were no more than thirty feet apart, and

though he kept most of his face hid beneath the thick collar of his coat, I saw his eyes go wide and his forehead wrinkle. He looked at me and Denny, likely wondering what we were doing up there, and when he did, I pushed up the brim of my hat and let him see my face.

Including the driver, there were eight of us, and while Driscoll had thirteen men, we all held shotguns. He should have let it go and surrendered, but he panicked. He grabbed for his gun, and his men followed his lead.

I wanted a shot at Driscoll, but a big man, gun in hand, jumped his horse right in front of me. I leveled the shotgun and pulled both triggers.

The double load of buckshot caught him in the chest, and his coat seemed to explode. He flew backward and hit the ground. Dropping the shotgun and drawing my Colt, I looked for Driscoll.

Guns were hammering all around me and half a dozen of his men were down, but then I saw Driscoll still on his horse. His face was a mask of blood, but his gun was still in his hand. Next to me, Estle Denny had his own Colt in his hand, and we fired at the same time. Driscoll's coat jerked with the impact, but his body didn't seem to react. His face hideous, Driscoll still tried to aim the Colt in his hand. Denny and I both fired just as Driscoll got off his shot. His bullet tore at the collar of my coat. Both our bullets struck home and Driscoll folded like a rag doll, sliding off his horse and into the bloodstained snow.

From first shot to last, I doubted more than thirty to forty seconds had passed, yet seven of their men lay dead or dying in the snow, and two others were wounded. At such close range the shotguns had simply torn them apart.

We came off lucky. One of the guards had a bullet in his leg, Sheriff Bullock had a mild crease along the back of his forearm, and Denny had a bloody line drawn on his ear by a bullet that had come too close.

We were already tidying things up when Owen and his

bunch came charging down the trail. He looked real disappointed when he saw the shooting was all over. "Could have saved a couple for us," he said. "That was a long, cold ride for nothing."

"Wish you'd have been here," I said. "You could've had my share, and welcome."

When the prisoners were ready and the dead men were tied across their saddles, Owen and his men started back for Deadwood. Denny and I went with them. I'd had enough of the trail, enough of the killing, and all I wanted was to take Mary Kay in my arms and never leave her again.

When we reached Deadwood I didn't waste a minute getting to the cabin. Mary Kay came into my arms, and for a long time I stood there holding her.

When I did let her go, I removed my coat and my gun belt. The coat I hung on a hook beside the door. My gun belt I rolled up and handed to Mary Kay. "Put it away somewhere safe," I said. "The good Lord willing, I don't ever intend to wear it again."

EPILOGUE

TWO years later my Colt still rests where Mary Kay put it that day. We've a fine ranch, the two of us, and our cattle are doing well. We also own half of a very good mercantile in Deadwood with Owen and Sarah, who married not long after the trouble with Driscoll.

Seeing Delmer Higgins's face when Sarah walked up and handed him the five hundred dollars was almost worth all the trouble we went through. But I'll say this for the man: while he figured to take advantage of Sarah, he couldn't help but grin a bit when she paid off.

There's been another change in our family, and that's another baby, a son named Taylor.

Mary Kay is more beautiful than ever, and I'm more in love with her than ever. There are wild, lonely trails still to be ridden, and every great once in a while I look at Cap and think about the way the high, lonesome country looks and feels on a warm spring day.

Those past trails are fine memories, but the memory of how Mary Kay looks and feels on a cold winter night is a much better one.

We've ridden our trails, Cap and me, and now someone else can ride them. Me, I intend to grow old, gray, and fat right here with Mary Kay.

If you have enjoyed this book and would like to receive details about other Walker Western titles, please write to:

Western Editor
Walker and Company
720 Fifth Avenue
New York, NY 10019